Girl TALK

Best Friends

BF

Have you seen all the Best Friends books?

1. Friends Forever
2. Oh Brother!
3. Spotlight on Sunita
4. A Challenge for Lauren
5. Gemma's Big Chance

GEMMA'S Big Chance

Sue Mongredien

First published in 1999 by BBC Worldwide Ltd
Woodlands, 80 Wood Lane, London W12 0TT

ISBN 0 563 55533 5

Cover photography by Jamie Hughes

Thanks to Empire

Printed and bound by Mackays of Chatham plc

Let Girl TALK introduce you to the greatest bunch of Best Friends ever...

First there's

Sunita

She's sussed out her brother

So has

Lauren

but things go horribly wrong...

Luckily

Gemma

is there for her best friend

leaving

Carli

to a shopping trip with

Anya

How are they going to get on?

Best Friends

Chapter 1

"Yeeeeesssss!"

Gemma Gordon put the phone down and did a mad dance around the living room. She was *finally* going to be helping out with the animals at the Paws Kennels and Cattery, every weekend, starting from next Saturday! For someone as totally animal-mad as Gemma, it was a dream come true.

Throwing herself on the old sofa, she grinned from ear to ear. When Ms Drury, Gemma's class teacher at Duston Middle School, had mentioned that her sister worked at the kennels, Gemma had seen her chance. She'd felt a bit shy asking Ms Drury about helping out there occasionally, but Lauren, her best friend, had egged her on.

"Go for it, Gemma," she'd told her. "You know

what they say – if you don't ask, you don't get!"

That might have been confident Lauren's motto, but Gemma wasn't usually one for putting herself forward. However, Ms Drury had asked her sister, Sheena, about taking on a helper – and Sheena had just called Gemma to ask her to come over to the kennels next weekend for a trial day helping out. Her last helper had recently left, so they had a slot for a new person. Talk about good timing! Gemma just *knew* that she and Sheena were going to get along great!

Gemma hopped off the sofa and went back to the phone. With such good news there was only one thing to do – let her best friends know all about it! After all, if it hadn't been for Lauren, she might never have dared ask in the first place.

She picked up the receiver and dialled Lauren's number. Lauren Standish was Gemma's next-door neighbour, as well as her best friend, and the two girls had known each other since they were babies.

Lauren answered the phone. She knew just what the news meant to her friend and squealed so loudly that Gemma had to hold the receiver away from her ear.

"Gems, that's fab!" Lauren said. "What will you be doing there? Don't tell me – cleaning up dog poo – I've heard that's a lovely job!"

Gemma giggled. "Yuck, I hope not. Listen – I can't talk long, you know what Dad's like. But I'll come round in a bit and tell you all about it!"

"You'd better!" said Lauren, as she rang off. Lauren was the kind of person who liked to know *everything*!

Sunita Banerjee was washing-up in the kitchen when the phone rang. She eyed the mountain of breakfast dishes with distaste and crossed her fingers under the water. 'Please let that be for me,' she said to herself, as her gran answered the call. Just because it was her mum's birthday today, Sunita didn't see why she had to do every single chore in the house – especially when she had two lazy brothers around, who didn't seem to understand the words 'fair share'.

"Sunita, *beti*!" called her grandmother from the hall. "It's Gemma for you!"

'Result!' thought Sunita. Hopefully she could get into a nice, long gossipy chat and by the time she'd finished, someone else would have done those pots.

"And don't be long," her grandmother told her, handing over the receiver. "There's a lot to do for the dinner party yet!"

Sunita sighed. Fat chance of her brothers ever lifting a finger. "Yes, *Dadima*," she muttered dutifully.

"Hi, Gems," she said into the phone. "What are you up to?... No way! Excellent! I knew they'd want you!"

Sunita was dying to get the full story, but one look at her gran waving the washing-up brush meaningfully stopped her from asking more. "Listen, Gemma," she sighed. "I can't chat long – it's Mum's birthday today and we're having a special dinner for her. And you know what *that* means."

"A house full of relatives and Sunita being a good little daughter?" Gemma laughed.

Sunita groaned. "That's about it! And right now, the good little daughter has a pile of lovely washing-up to get back to. Looks like I'll have to wait until tomorrow for the details. You're still coming round, aren't you? Tell me all about it, then."

Gemma smiled as she put the phone down. Of her best friends, there were just Anya Michaels and Carli Pike left to tell. Carli wasn't on the phone, but luckily she was due round at the Gordons' house that afternoon – Gemma reckoned she could

just about wait till then to tell her the news! In the meantime, she'd ring Anya, then go and fill in Mum! Mum already knew she'd asked her teacher about it, and thought her working at the kennels was a great idea.

Anya was the only person so far who wasn't madly excited for Gemma. "Oh, right," she said, when Gemma told her the gossip. "And you *want* to do that, do you? Or is it for a Brownie badge or something?"

Anya couldn't really see the point of doing any work for fun. Unlike the rest of the gang, her parents were quite well-off and Anya had all the money she wanted to spend on herself. Fun, in Anya's opinion, was shopping, shopping, and then a bit more shopping for luck.

"And what if you catch a horrible disease, or fleas?" she asked.

Gemma laughed and rolled her eyes, just picturing Anya turning up her delicate nose at the thought. "I'm not going to catch a horrible disease from looking after a few cats and dogs!" she told her friend. "It's going to be brilliant – honestly!"

"Yeah, right! Taking care of a load of smelly animals sounds *sooo* much fun, I might have to join you!"

"Yeah, course you will, Anya," Gemma teased.

"Can't see you getting your Nike Airs covered in mucky cat litter, somehow!"

"Ha, ha! Are you going to Sunita's tomorrow, by the way?"

"Yeah, I've just spoken to her."

"OK, I'll see you there," Anya said. Then there was a pause. "Hey, Gems, I'm pleased for you really, you know..."

Gemma smiled as she put down the phone. Just then, her dad came in, looking almost as chuffed as she was feeling. He had a big, yummy-smelling carrier bag from the chip shop and waved it in the air. "Grub's up!" he called. "We're celebrating, Gems!"

'Too right we are,' thought Gemma. But what was *he* so happy about? Curious, Gemma followed her dad into the kitchen. Garry Gordon was normally pretty cheerful, but today he seemed in an even better mood than usual. She watched him plonk the bag of lunchtime chips on the worktop, then grab Mum around the waist and swing her into the air.

"Garry!" she squealed, laughing at him. "What's got into you?"

"Megabucks!" he said, grinning. "That's what's got into me! We got the Branksome deal! All two hundred cars of it!"

Gemma stared in amazement as her parents started acting like five-year-olds, whooping and cheering in the kitchen. Honestly, sometimes she wondered who the real children *were* in this house. What had her dad said? The Branksome deal… she seemed to remember him talking about it over tea the other week. Garry Gordon ran a small garage in the arches by the railway station, and Gemma knew a deal for servicing two hundred cars was something pretty special. It could mean a *lot* of extra money for the family.

"Just think, Lucy," he was saying to Gemma's sister, who'd run in from the garden to see what all the noise was about. "We'll be able to splash out on a flash holiday this year!" Gemma and Lucy laughed as he started singing: "'Oh, we're off to sunny Spain…!' Eh, kids?"

"That's great news, Garry," Mrs Gordon was saying, unwrapping the parcels of chips. "Come on, let's tuck in. Fish for you, Lucy, veggie nuggets for Gems…"

They all sat at the table, munching and talking excitedly.

"Can I have a pony, Dad?" asked Lucy, wide-eyed.

Garry Gordon laughed, almost choking on a sausage. "I'm not loaded yet, Luce!" he told his youngest daughter. "How about a donkey ride on our holiday, instead?"

That reminded Gemma of *her* good news. "You're not the only one who's got some extra work, Dad," she said proudly. "I've gone and got myself a job, too – helping out at the Paws kennels – you know, the ones over Maryland way. They want me to start there next Saturday!" It all came out in a muddle, she was so excited.

Gemma's mum smiled at her. "That's great, love! That's really exciting. But –" She looked over at her husband.

"Mmm, well done, Gems," said Mr Gordon, but his voice didn't sound quite right. He put his fork down on his plate and cleared his throat.

Gemma looked at him expectantly. *Uh-oh*. If her dad had stopped eating, this could only be serious.

"The thing is," he said, "me and your mum are going to need you to help us out while this big job goes through. We'll need you to keep an eye on Lucy at the arches, while we're both working there on Saturdays – maybe even on Sundays." He tried to catch her eye. "Be a bit of extra pocket money for you, and all... What do you reckon? Can this kennels thing wait a couple of months?"

Gemma gulped and stared at him. Whatever she'd been expecting her dad to say, it certainly hadn't been that. "Well, no," she said, shaking her head. "Not really. Their last helper's just moved away, so they've got room for me *now*. If I don't take the place up, then..."

"I'm sure I can have a word with the owners," said Mrs Gordon, trying to be soothing. "I'm sure they'll understand when I explain the situation."

Gemma swallowed. This wasn't how things were meant to turn out. "Well, I've already told them I'll do it," she said. A funny feeling was starting in her stomach. "I mean – I've already said yes. I can't really change the arrangement now, can I?"

"Well, you might have to," said her dad bluntly. He shrugged. "Sorry, love, but this contract is one in a million. We absolutely *have* to do a cracking job for these blokes – otherwise we won't see their money again. So, I'm sorry, but that's just the way it is."

Gemma bit her lip and turned to her mum. "Can't Lauren's mum look after Lucy?" she asked, feeling a pleading note creep into her voice. "Just on Saturdays – I mean, I can look after her on Sundays..."

Mary Gordon looked over at her husband, feeling sorry for Gemma. She knew that working at Paws would be like Christmas every week for her animal-loving daughter. "It's just that you're so

good with Lucy, Gems," she said, putting an arm around her. "You'd *really* be helping us out."

"Who says she's good with me?" muttered Lucy, sticking her tongue out the side of her mouth.

Garry Gordon was sympathetic but firm. "Gemma," he said, "I just said no, didn't I? Karen Standish has more than enough children of her own to cope with. I know you're disappointed but there's nothing else for it. And that's my last word on the subject." He picked up his knife and fork again and carried on eating, spearing a chip as if he meant business.

"But, Dad –"

"I said, *no*! Now, I don't want to hear another word about it!" Her dad's voice hadn't quite reached a shout, but Gemma knew he was about to lose his temper any second if she pushed it further.

A tear suddenly plopped onto her plate, then another. He was so unfair! He was so, *so* unfair! The funny feeling in her stomach got tighter and tighter.

"What's Paws, Mum?" asked Lucy.

That was the last straw for Gemma. She pushed her plate away and her face crumpled up in tears as she raced out the room, pelting upstairs.

Paws! She didn't want to hear that word! How could Dad be so mean? She *hated* him!

Gemma threw herself down on her bed and clutched her pillow, sobbing into it as if her heart would break.

Chapter 2

"Happy birthday!"

"Happy birthday!"

Indranee Banerjee was opening her presents after a delicious lunch. The Banerjees' living room was packed with aunts, uncles and cousins, who'd all come to Northborough to celebrate with her.

"How lovely!" Mrs Banerjee exclaimed, as she unwrapped a carved wooden elephant from her sister. "Thank you, Kamini! It's wonderful!"

"It's for luck," Auntie Kamini told her. "Not that you need it, Indranee! Well, not by the look of that glitzy parcel that's heading your way!"

She smiled at Sunita who was passing her gift over the table. Sunita had spent ages wrapping it in silver paper and making the purple ribbon round it go twirly at the ends. Carli had shown her the trick with a pair of scissors, and the present

now looked fantastic.

"Goodness!" smiled her mother. "Sunny, this must have taken ages!"

"She's such a clever little girl!" beamed Sunita's gran, proudly.

Sunita wrinkled her nose in reply. Sometimes her gran seemed to think she was still a toddler, rather than ten years old! "Open it up, Mum," she urged.

"Such a shame to spoil this paper," Mrs Banerjee murmured, as her slender fingers carefully unwrapped the parcel. She pulled the paper off to reveal a silky honey-coloured scarf that Sunita had spent ages sewing hundreds of tiny golden beads on to, in graceful swirling patterns. Sunita loved designing and making clothes – it was her dream one day to become a successful fashion designer. People told her she had a real knack for making anything look great!

"Sunny!" Even her mother, who knew how talented her daughter was, was surprised at the intricate patterns she'd created. "This is just gorgeous!" She put it carefully around her neck at once, and smiled across at her daughter. "I love it! Thank you, darling. It's going to be my best scarf."

Sunita blushed. "It suits you," she said.

"It certainly does," Mrs Chopra told her. "Will

you make me one for my birthday, Sunita?" she asked, leaning over the table and winking at Sunita.

"Sunita's a very busy girl, you know!" her protective gran put in firmly. Old Mrs Banerjee knew just how long the scarf had taken her granddaughter, and more to the point, if anyone else was going to get their hands on one of Sunita's scarves, it would be *her*! Although she was usually quite strict with Sunita, Mrs Banerjee didn't mind so much the time she spent sewing. After all, it was far more gentle than some of the dreadful things her friends got up to. That Lauren girl, for instance. She was always out playing football!

"Of course, Sunita's studies are excellent, too!" Mr Banerjee couldn't resist putting in. "She's going to be an accountant, you know! My daughter's good at everything!"

Sunita blushed furiously. Uh-oh, on to Dad's favourite subject – her future career! Why on earth he seemed to think she could become an accountant – or that she would even *want* to be one, more to the point – was totally beyond Sunita.

"In fact, her teacher was only telling me at the last parents' evening, 'Sunita Banerjee is going to go far...' she said, and..."

'Go far' was about right – Sunita reckoned it was time to go far away from Dad before he came out with any more of this talk! Grabbing a pile of empty dishes, she escaped from her place at the table. "I'll start clearing up," she muttered as she left the room.

Her gran had already gone into the kitchen and was nattering to a couple of friends about something or other when Sunita walked in. They were talking in Hindi, which meant that Sunita could only understand the odd word – and just to make it worse, her grandmother always made it really obvious if she was discussing something especially juicy. Now, for example, she was looking furtively around the room to check who could hear her, hunching forward slightly and lowering her voice. All very mysterious!

As Sunita started to scrape the left-over food into the bin, she heard her brother Vikram's name mentioned. Her ears pricked up automatically. What were they saying about him that was so hush-hush?

Sunita strained her ears so hard they almost started aching, but she couldn't recognise more than the most basic word. *Idhar* – that meant 'here', and then Gran said 'June' in English, which was next month. Apart from that, the only other thing she picked up was the name 'Jamila' that was mentioned a couple of times.

Sunita frowned in annoyance. What were they saying about her brother and this 'Jamila' person? Then a thought suddenly struck her and she almost dropped a plate into the bin in shock. Surely they weren't hatching plans for her brother and this Jamila? Plans like…

"Sunita!"

Her grandmother's sharp voice broke through her thoughts and Sunita spun round, blushing at being caught trying to eavesdrop.

"You're going to scrape the pattern off that plate in a minute, Sunita!" sharp-eyed Mrs Banerjee said, raising her eyebrows at her granddaughter. "Why don't you pass the drinks round again? People will be getting thirsty out there!"

Sunita obediently put the plate on the side and left the room, her head in a whirl. Could Gran and her cronies really be talking about what she *thought* they were?

"Go away," Gemma muttered when she heard a knock on her bedroom door. She sniffed loudly, still lying on her bed, clutching the soggy pillow. The door opened a crack and her mum put her head round.

"Can I come in?"

"No," sniffed Gemma, not wanting to talk about Paws or garages or her wretched little sister. What was the point?

Mary Gordon ignored her daughter's answer and sat on the bed next to her, stroking Gemma's thick brown hair. "Oh, love," she said, soothingly. "It's bad timing, isn't it? You and Dad both getting your dream jobs on the same day..."

"Yeah, but Dad gets to keep his, doesn't he?" Gemma muttered, sticking her lip out and staring at the pillow. "Unlike me." She knew she was being unfair, she knew it wasn't her mum's fault, but she felt so horrible and cross inside, she couldn't just switch it off and pretend to be OK.

Her mum smoothed Gemma's hair off her face. "Look, Gems, once Dad's calmed down, I'll talk to him. See if we can work something out, eh?" She bent down and kissed Gemma's hot head. "Trust me!"

Gemma tried to smile up at her, but her heart wasn't really in it. She couldn't see her dad backing down now – not over his precious garage!

She sat up, suddenly remembering Lauren, and how she'd promised to go round there after lunch. Her happy-go-lucky friend would be the best person to cheer her up right now – if anyone could

make her feel better, it was Lauren.

Five minutes later, Carli Pike was knocking at the Gordons' front door. Carli loved animals too, but pets weren't allowed on the Fairlight estate where she lived. Kind-hearted Gemma had suggested the solution: Thumper, Gemma's rabbit, loved company and so Carli could keep her own pet rabbit – pretty, white-furred Snowball – in a hutch next door to his! Carli loved having a pet of her own. She often popped round to cuddle Snowball after school or to clean out her hutch.

Going round to the Gordons' house was a pleasure for Carli – they were such a friendly family that even someone as shy as her felt at home there.

Lucy answered the door, acting all grown-up.

"Gemma's not here," she told Carli importantly. "She's crying because Dad's making her look after me. But I don't want her to anyway! I want Kate, our babysitter to, but Dad says it's up to the family. Anyway, Gemma ran out and left all her chips!"

Carli was a bit taken aback by this barrage of information. Luckily, her sister Annie was roughly the same age as Lucy, so she knew how to read between the lines. "So where's Gemma, now?" she asked quickly, as Lucy looked on the verge of launching into another news broadcast.

"Next door. Dad's dead cross. He said –"

"Thanks, Lucy," said Carli hastily, before the seven-year-old went into any more gory details. Then she dashed round to the Standishes, mind racing. What was going on? Gemma was always so cheerful, something really terrible must have happened to upset her!

As she entered Lauren's bedroom, she found a hiccuping, red-eyed Gemma in the middle of telling the whole story. "There's no way he'll let me do it now," she was saying miserably. "He's made his mind up that we've all got to help out on this job."

As usual, Lauren was in her tracksuit and a pair of trainers, looking as if she was just about to run a four-minute mile. Knowing Lauren, she'd probably been out running before *breakfast*. Right now though, all of her energy was going into telling Gemma just what she thought of Mr Gordon.

"Well, tell him to stuff his job!" she was saying indignantly, hands on her hips. "Not your problem, is it? You should just go to the kennels like you said you would – it's up to him to find someone to look after Lucy!"

"What's happened?" asked Carli, shocked to see how upset Gemma was looking.

Gemma told her first the good news she'd had from Paws, followed by the bad news she'd had from her dad.

"Parents, eh!" Lauren moaned, tossing her long blonde ponytail impatiently. "Just tell him no. This is your big chance, Gems! This is what you've always wanted to do!"

"I know," said Gemma sadly, trying to be fair about it. "But this is my dad's big chance, too. He wants *this* work as much as I want *my* work. I don't know what to do!"

Lauren snorted. "Dads are a nightmare!" she announced loudly, folding her arms across her chest. Then she caught Carli's eye, and blushed with embarrassment. "Oh – sorry, Carli."

Carli shrugged. Her dad had left them two years ago and it still felt sore to think about it. She felt herself going red – partly thinking about him, and partly because she disagreed with what Lauren was saying about Gemma's problem.

"Don't worry about it," she managed to say.

There was an awkward silence. "Any bright ideas, Carli?" Gemma asked to change the subject.

"Lauren says to stuff my dad's job. What do you think?"

"If you ask me, you're lucky to have your dads around, both of you," Carli said. "I wish I still did!"

She sounded so angry that Lauren caught her hands and gave them an apologetic squeeze. "Oh, Carli," she said. "I didn't mean to upset you! Me and my big mouth!"

Carli sat on the bed. "Don't worry, Lauren, I know what you mean – dads *can* be a nightmare, sometimes, and I should know! But families ought to stick together and help each other out, that's what I think. I'd do anything for my dad if it meant he'd come home again." She thought for a second. "Why not try and find someone else to look after Lucy, Gemma?"

Lauren snorted. "You think she'd find anyone mad enough to say yes?"

Gemma groaned. "Yeah, they'd have to be a real sucker to want to look after *that* brat!"

"Or deaf, so they wouldn't be able to hear the whingeing," said Lauren with a shudder.

Gemma's face fell. "So, Lauren, I take it you wouldn't be a volunteer to look after her, would you?"

"Me? No way!" blurted Lauren. "Sorry, Gems, but I've got swimming practice every week – Peter will kill me if I miss it..." She shrugged. "Besides, I'd probably strangle her after five minutes..."

"That's true," Gemma admitted. She turned hesitantly to the small blonde girl beside her. "Carli? I don't suppose..."

Carli's green eyes were apologetic through her thick glasses. "Oh, Gemma, I wish I could, but weekends are the only time me and Annie really get to see Dad. You know how it is..."

"Don't I just," groaned Gemma. She rolled over on Lauren's bed, sighing heavily. "What am I going to do?"

"Don't worry," said Carli. "We'll think of something. Between us, Sunita and Anya, we're bound to think of a way round the problem."

"And don't forget, we'll do whatever we can," said Lauren, firmly, giving Gemma a nudge and offering her a little finger.

The three of them linked hands and said their secret oath together:

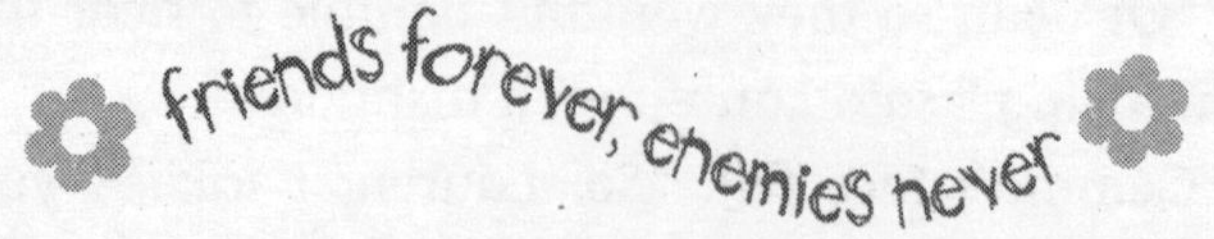

"Now, let's have a smile from Miss Gordon!" ordered Lauren. "We'll get you to Paws if it's the last thing we do!"

Gemma smiled gratefully at them. She knew that her friends would always be there for her, but for the first time in her life, she was starting to wonder if that would be enough…

On Sunday morning, the Banerjee home was starting to get back to normal after the big get-together the night before. The guests had all gone, leaving behind them a heap of presents for Indranee and a stack of dirty dishes that Sunita seemed to have ended up with.

She was just putting away the last clean plate from the dishwasher when her grandmother came into the kitchen, beaming to see everything so clean and tidy.

"You are a good girl, Sunita, *beti*!" she told her briskly, opening the fridge to get a carton of milk. "Let's have a cup of tea and I'll tell you all about the good idea I've had for you."

Sunita's eyebrows shot up. This sounded like trouble. Last time her gran had had one of her so-called good ideas, it had meant extra maths tuition for Sunita – which was an extremely *bad* idea in her opinion!

"OK, *Dadima,*" said Sunita, using her pet name for her grandmother in an attempt to soften her up.

The kettle clicked itself off and old Mrs Banerjee poured the boiling water into an ancient brown teapot. Sunita, meanwhile, waited expectantly to hear what her grandmother had to say *this* time.

"Sunita, we're pleased you're growing up over here," the old lady began, her sharp brown eyes fixed on her granddaughter the whole time. "You're doing well at school, you have made some nice friends and we're proud of you. One day I am sure you will be a fine Indian lady, just like your mother."

Sunita gulped. She wasn't used to such praise from her strict grandmother. Where was all of this leading?

"I know you have some English ways," Mrs Banerjee continued with a sigh. "Those jeans you girls all wear and some of that music you listen to on the radio. But I don't want my Sunny to be *too* English; I want her to get to know her own Hindi culture, and be proud of it, as I am. That is why –"

"But I *am* proud of it!" Sunita said quickly, not sure what Mrs Banerjee had in mind, but pretty

certain she wasn't going to like it.

"That is why," her grandmother repeated, ignoring the interruption, "I've arranged for you to have Hindi lessons, so you can learn your language and become a proper Indian girl."

Sunita stared at her in a stunned silence. "But Gran, I'm so busy with all my homework, I don't know if I'll have time for any more lessons..." she started desperately.

Mrs Banerjee clicked her teeth. "Nonsense! A few hours a week extra won't make any difference! Besides, you'll enjoy it. Hindi is a beautiful language – you should be pleased that I am giving you the chance to learn it!"

Sunita stared at the old lady in horror. "But does it have to be lessons? Maybe I can learn from you and Mum – I've already picked up some words, Gran..."

Mrs Banerjee would not be moved. "'Some words' doesn't mean you know a language, Sunny," she told her firmly. "And anyway, I've already arranged it. Auntie Rita is going to take you – starting from next Saturday."

Saturday? This was getting worse by the minute! Sunita liked to spend Saturdays with her friends, or working on her latest fashion design. "But –" Sunita started, just as her brother Vikram walked in.

"Would you like a cup of tea?" Mrs Banerjee asked her grandson, considering the matter closed.

Sunita scowled. Great! More studying – just what she didn't want! But Vikram had reminded her of something – the conversation the old ladies had been having in the kitchen the night before. Just a minute... if she knew Hindi, it would mean she would be able to understand *all* the secret gossip in the future. She'd never have to miss out on any news again!

A smile started to break across Sunita's face. Maybe these lessons weren't such a bad idea, after all...

Later that day, Lauren called for Gemma and the two of them made their way over to Sunita's house. The Banerjees only lived three streets away, which made it easy for the three girls to see a lot of each other.

"Sunita told me her dad's letting us watch the latest Disney video," Gemma told Lauren. "It only came into the shop yesterday – cool, eh?"

"Nice one!" said Lauren, although she tended to prefer films with lots of action and death-defying stunts. "Hey – have you thought about asking

Sunita to look after Lucy on Saturdays? She gets on OK with her, doesn't she?"

"She does, you're right," agreed Gemma. "But Mum's managed to talk Dad round a bit..."

"So you *can* go to Paws after all!" yelled Lauren delightedly. "Brilliant, Gems!"

"Not quite," Gemma said, laughing despite herself at her enthusiastic friend. "I'm going to spend one Saturday at Paws, then the next one looking after Lucy, then Paws, then Lucy – so it's every other week at least, which is something."

"Better than nothing!" Lauren agreed.

Anya and Carli were already round at Sunita's by the time Lauren and Gemma arrived. Sunita waved the Disney video at them as they came into the living room. "Check it out!" she called across the room. "I'm in Dad's good books for sure!"

"How come?" Lauren wanted to know. "Joined the 'Junior Accountants Club'?"

"That'll be the day," Sunita groaned. "No – I've agreed to have some Hindi lessons. Learn to be a 'proper Indian girl', as Gran put it."

"Extra lessons?" exclaimed Anya in horror, almost choking on the samosa she'd been nibbling. "Are you mad?"

"Well, that's what I thought too, at first," Sunita said mysteriously.

"What, and then you had a brain transplant?" Lauren joked. She was with Anya on this one – what could be good about extra lessons?

"No – then I realised the amazing gossip potential involved," laughed Sunita. "I'll get to find out everything my gran's saying – all those juicy secrets! It's going to be great, understanding what they're all talking about – especially when it's about Vikram!"

Lauren looked up at the mention of Sunita's brother. "Don't tell me – Liverpool want to give him a trial!" she asked, only half-joking. He was such a brilliant, talented player, Lauren thought anything was possible. A keen football player herself, she really admired him.

"Oh no, nothing about boring football," Sunita said dismissively. "Far juicier – we're talking Vikram's love-life, here!"

"His love-life?" It was the last thing Lauren had been thinking of. "What do you mean?"

Sunita told them about the conversation she'd heard the day before. "They kept mentioning his name, right. Plus, someone called Jamila and the fact that she's going to be over here next month."

She gazed around the circle of friends, who were all staring blankly back at her. "Don't you get it? I think they're talking about arranging his marriage!"

"His *marriage*?" Anya squealed. "Do you think so? He's only fifteen!"

"No way!" breathed Gemma. "An arranged marriage? Are your mum and dad really into that sort of thing?"

"Sunny, you'll be able to design the wedding outfits!" said Carli, excitedly.

"Will they be arranging one for you as well, one day?" Anya said, horrified at the thought.

The only person who wasn't saying anything was Lauren. Her mouth had fallen open in surprise and, quick as a flash, Anya popped the last corner of her samosa into it. Lauren's eyes nearly jumped out of her head in shock.

"Anya! What are you playing at?" she spluttered, spraying bits of food everywhere.

"Sorry," giggled Anya. "I thought you'd lost the plot for a minute – just wanted to bring you back down to earth!"

"Well, next time try saying something," snapped Lauren. Her mind was reeling with the news about Vikram. *Married*! She couldn't believe it. It wasn't as if she liked him in that way herself, she hated all boys, didn't she? It was just a bit of a shock, that was all. She was used to Vikram on the footy pitch, not Vikram the husband!

"Ooh, you've gone red," Anya teased, poking Lauren in the ribs. "Ooh, look at Lauren – do you know what, girls? I think she's jealous of Jamila! I think she fancies Vikram herself!"

"I do not!" Lauren said loudly, feeling herself grow even more red in the face. "He's all right, but still a stupid boy!"

"Too right," said Sunita. "And I should know."

"Why've you gone red, then?" Anya persisted. "Hasn't she gone red?"

"She has," Carli and Gemma said together.

"Look, are we going to watch this video, or what?" said Lauren crossly. "Honestly, you're like a bunch of gossipy old grannies, you lot!"

The others burst into giggles at their red-faced friend, who was brandishing the video box angrily at them.

"Mmm... touchy!" said Anya, winking.

Lauren was about to reply, but Carli beat her to it. "What's the latest with your dad, Gems?" she asked quickly. She hated being teased herself and could see Lauren was really squirming. Mind you, Lauren was usually the first to be winding up someone, so it was quite cool to see her have to handle it for a change!

Gemma had to go through the whole story again for the benefit of Sunita and Anya, who hadn't even known about the problems she'd faced from her parents. "But hopefully, if I'm doing a week on, a week off, it won't be so bad," she finished. "And I still get to work with all those lovely cats and dogs!"

"Parents can be a real pain," said Sunita. "At least you haven't got a gran like mine, butting in as well!"

"They just don't get it, do they?" Anya moaned. "Take my dad, for instance. I hardly see him at the moment, he's so busy with work and I *really* need some new clothes – I mean, I'm desperate! Astrid's ice-skating party's coming up and I *must* have a new outfit – and what does he say? He's too busy to take me shopping! Why does he work such long hours if he can't enjoy the money he earns by spending it on me?"

"What, you reckon he enjoys traipsing round town with you, spending all his hard-earned dosh on your clothes, do you?" Lauren said, unable to resist a dig in return for all the grief Anya had just given her. "Doesn't sound like much fun to me!"

"We don't *all* want to live in a smelly tracksuit, Lauren!" Anya flashed back, haughtily.

"What's this party then?" Gemma put in quickly. At this rate, Lauren and Anya were going to have a bust-up!

Anya preened herself. "Well, it's Astrid's birthday, and you know what good friends me and Astrid are..."

The other four exchanged amused glances. Anya went to Lady Margaret Regis, a private school in town, instead of the local school that they all went to. They'd been told all about this super-trendy girl, Astrid, and how she and Anya were great friends. Unfortunately, the others had since found out that Astrid didn't quite see Anya in the same light. That was something Anya chose to forget!

"She's having an ice-skating party," Anya continued, "and it's bound to be pretty flashy. Anyway, she's asked a couple of people – including *me* of course – so I need to get something really cool to wear. I mean, I've got to look the part, haven't I?"

"I've got a smelly old tracksuit you can borrow if you want..." Lauren teased.

Anya tossed back her straight, dark hair crossly, and was just about to launch into a smart retort when Mr Banerjee put his head around the door.

"Not watching the video then, girls?" he asked.

"All we can hear is chat, chat, chat!"

"We're just about to," Sunita said, grateful for an interruption. "Thanks, Dad!"

"Here's another idea!" Lauren said, gurgling with laughter. "There's always my footy kit –" She broke off as a cushion from Anya hit her squarely in the face. "Aaaargh!"

Gemma found herself laughing harder than she'd done for ages. Her friends were so mad, no one could stay miserable for long around them!

Chapter 4

"Astrid! Over here! I've saved you a seat!"

For all Anya's confident words on Sunday, she was actually on a major mission the next day at school: to get into Astrid's good books and wangle herself an invite to the ice-skating party. Even though she'd told her friends that Astrid had already invited her, it wasn't actually true – yet!

Astrid smiled at Anya as she took her seat, and Anya glowed with importance. Astrid was so popular and cool, an invite to her party would really secure Anya a place with the in-crowd!

Anya lost interest in the morning assembly, and started thinking instead of exactly what she was going to wear to the party – when Astrid finally got round to inviting her. What did professional skaters wear, anyway? Those all-in-one outfits...

no way! How about something a bit prettier? One of those frilly little skating skirts, with thick tights? She'd look the part, all right, but might feel a bit of an idiot if everyone else was in jeans. She'd have to get it just right...

"And today I'd like to introduce Miss Fairley, who's going to be teaching class 6 while Mrs Monroe is on maternity leave," droned Miss Hamilton, the head teacher. "Please show her that the Lady Margaret girls know how to behave impeccably!"

There were a few sniggers, but Anya brightened suddenly, and sat up straight in her chair to get a better look. Miss Fairley was tall and slim with a short red bob... and was wearing wicked black velvet trousers. Yes – that was it! Anya was sure she'd seen a similar pair in the new clothes shop in the High Street. They were exactly what Anya wanted to be wearing to the ice-rink – *when* she was invited! Now all she had to do was talk her dad into taking her on a shopping spree...

As the week went by, though, Anya seemed to find it more difficult than ever to pin her dad down. One night he was staying away on a training course, then he was having a business dinner with clients – then he was too tired to do anything other than fall asleep in front of the TV! By the time Thursday came around, Anya had called an emergency meeting at her place after school – this was turning out to be a total crisis!

"I mean, I've just *got* to get those trousers!" she whined to the others. "What am I going to do?"

"Wear something else?" Lauren yawned. She hated talking about clothes – it was so boring! "Anyone fancy a game of something? Don't suppose Christopher's left his Playstation over here has he?"

"No, thank goodness!" Anya snapped. She didn't get on with her half-brother very well at the best of times, and she disliked his Playstation even more. "Last time he was here, I had to keep watching *EastEnders* on the portable, while he blipped away on that awful machine!"

"What's up, Gems?" Sunita asked, noticing how quiet their friend was being.

Gemma pulled a gloomy face. "Oh, just Dad," she said. "He's being a bit funny with me, I think. I know he's cross with me for not mucking in down at the garage... He's got this real thing about families all sticking together and he keeps going on about it. Talk about a guilt trip! I'm almost

wishing I'd never heard of Paws Kennels – then life would be nice and normal!"

"Yeah, but then you'd have missed out on your big chance," Carli put in, practically. "I'm sure once you start helping out at Paws, it'll be worth all the aggro your dad's giving you."

"I suppose so," said Gemma, brightening a bit. "Hey, I hadn't realised, but there's a vet's surgery right next door to the kennels! I mean, I knew they were close to each other, but my mum drove round there the other night to meet Sheena, and she said they're actually right next door!"

"Cool!" said Sunita. The girls all knew it had always been Gemma's long-standing ambition to be a vet. "That'll be great! Are you going to go over and introduce yourself? You might be able to help *them* out, too!"

"In my dreams!" Gemma smiled.

"Look, that's all very well," said Anya peevishly. "But what about me? We haven't sorted out *my* problem yet!"

"I hardly think the absence of a new pair of trousers in your wardrobe is in the same league as Gemma's grief, Anya," Lauren pointed out, blunt as ever.

"My Aunty Michelle loves shopping," Carli said timidly. "I'm sure she'd take you, if you really wanted her to?"

Anya was just about to turn her nose up at Carli's offer, when she suddenly noticed Gemma's steely blue eyes, sending her a warning look. "Er..." she stammered, lost for words under her friend's fierce gaze. "Erm, yes, great, Carli, that would be very nice. Thanks. I'm sure it'll be fun."

Carli smiled. "I'll see what I can do," she promised, turning slightly pink.

Inside her head, Anya groaned. What had she let herself in for? As far as she could remember, Carli's Aunt Michelle was a bit dippy – she wouldn't know fashion if she fell over it! Anya shuddered at the thought. She would have to get out of this arrangement as quickly as possible!

By the time Saturday morning finally came around, Gemma was so thrilled about her first day at Paws that she could hardly eat her breakfast.

"Come on, love," Mrs Gordon teased her. "That toast is for eating, not looking at! I know I spread the jam on beautifully, but you can put it in your mouth, you know, I won't be offended!"

Gemma beamed at her. "Sorry, Mum," she said. "I'm just so..."

Her mum ruffled her hair. "I know you are," she told her. "And so you should be! It's not every day your dream job comes along, is it?"

Mr Gordon appeared in the kitchen, in his usual overalls. He looked tired – he'd been working extra hard for the last week, as one of his mechanics was off sick. Mum had helped out with the administration as much as she possibly could, but there was still an awful lot to be done before the job was over.

"The big day!" he said, helping himself to a cup of tea. "All set, then? I'll give you a lift into town if you're quick."

Gemma blinked in surprise. "Are you sure?" she said. "I was going to take my bike..."

Mr Gordon put a friendly hand on his daughter's shoulder. "Of course I'm sure," he said gruffly. "Don't want to be late for your first day, now, do you?"

Mrs Gordon gave a secret wink to her daughter while Mr Gordon had a quick slurp of tea. Maybe her dad was coming around to the idea of Gemma being at the kennels after all!

Gemma's excitement suddenly turned to nerves once she was in the car. What if Sheena didn't like

her? Or what if the *animals* didn't like her? And what if she made an awful mistake and they didn't want her to come back again?

Mr Gordon caught sight of his daughter's face. "You'll be great," he told her. "You're Garry Gordon's daughter, aren't you? Of course you're going to be great!"

Gemma smiled nervously as they pulled into the drive shared by the kennels and the vet's surgery. It was really one huge red-brick house split into two – the vet's on the left, with the little plaque by the door, and the kennels on the right, with a big sign at the front. Gemma could hear the barking dogs before she'd even opened the car door, and found herself feeling excited again.

Mr Gordon looked at his watch. "We're a few minutes early – OK if we pop in to see Matt Jamison, next door?"

"Fine," said Gemma. She'd met the vet once before, when Thumper had to have his injections, and knew that he and Dad went to the same pub.

"Morning, Matt," Mr Gordon said, as they walked into the reception area. "Don't worry, mate, nothing's wrong with the rabbit, just thought I'd say hello. You've met our Gemma, haven't you? Well, she's going to be helping out next door on the odd Saturday, so you'll probably

be seeing her around the place."

Matt Jamison was tall, dark-haired and friendly-looking. Gemma managed a smile, even though she was feeling shy and nervous all over again.

"Helping out next door, eh?" Matt said. "Lucky old Sheena! How come she gets all the good helpers, then?"

Gemma's eyes lit up as an idea immediately came into her head. "Dad, do you think I could – " she started to say, but Mr Gordon was just a bit too quick for her.

"Oh, no, you don't," he said with a laugh, reading Gemma's mind. "One Saturday in two is enough for you right now, madam – if that's what you were going to ask!" He turned to Matt. "We've got a huge order on at the arches right now, so I'm up to my eyes in it. And you, young lady, are needed back home when you're not here, so don't get any ideas about any more work, OK?"

Matt laughed. "Well, I won't keep you," he said. "You must be dying to get started!"

"Oh, I am," Gemma breathed, excitedly. "I think I'm really going to enjoy myself here!"

She did, too. Once Dad had driven off, the first thing Sheena did was to make Gemma some orange squash and break open a packet of Kit-Kats. Sheena looked a bit older than Gemma's teacher and was comfortingly big and friendly. The sunny kitchen was full of pictures of cats and dogs, and Sheena's own dog, a big, soppy labrador called Harvey, lay at her feet, gazing up at his mistress adoringly.

"Now then," Sheena said. "I'm afraid we can't give you anything too exciting to do here – I can't really let you walk the dogs until I know that I can trust you with them, and half of them are probably bigger than you, anyway! But I'd love you to help me with some of the feeding and grooming, as well as cleaning out the kennels, too! *And* of course, the most important part of the job..."

"What's that?" asked Gemma nervously, hoping it wouldn't be anything too difficult.

"Well, we want to make the animals happy, don't we? They're away from their owners and are sometimes frightened or lonely. So it would *really* help me if you could make a fuss of some of the animals. Just so they feel that they've got a friend here, you know?"

Gemma could hardly speak, she was so thrilled. A whole day, playing with animals, and that would be helping out! It was even better than she thought!

Sheena smiled at Gemma's excited face. "Great!" she said. "Well, I'd better introduce you to some of our residents, then, hadn't I?"

"Oh, it was *fantastic*!" Gemma said, beaming as she shovelled baked beans on to her fork. Back home after her first day at the kennels, she felt as if she was about to burst with happiness.

Mrs Gordon smiled at her daughter who was practically glowing. "Come on, then, tell us all about it," she said.

Gemma swallowed a mouthful of food quickly, hardly tasting it. "Well, there are about fourteen dog kennels out in the yard – they've got all sorts of dogs there, a Great Dane and everything! Then there are a couple of collies, brother and sister, really barky and bouncy and a Jack Russell, Archie, he's sweet, and a Labrador, a spaniel, oh, and there's an Alsatian puppy who's really silly and cute…"

"And what were you doing with the dogs?" her mother put in, to give Gemma a second or two to take a breath. "Feeding them or walking them or what?"

Gemma was just about to answer, when they heard the phone crash down in the other room. Mr Gordon walked in, looking gloomy. "That was Jerry," he said, folding his arms across his chest. "Going to be off for another couple of weeks, the doctor said. Complete rest – can't put any strain on his back at all. So we're *really* stuck now. I'll have to ring round, see if any of the other lads can work extra." He sighed, looking tired and fed up, then turned to Lucy. "And next weekend, madam, I don't want any more bad behaviour from you!"

Lucy's bottom lip started quivering and her face went red. "I was bored!" she whined. "I hate it down there, smelly old arches!"

"Lucy!" snapped Mrs Gordon, and suddenly Gemma noticed how tired her mum was looking, too.

Lucy stared at her plate, and stabbed sulkily at a sausage.

Gemma's heart sank. She finished off her beans and mash, then washed up the pots without even being asked. She hated feeling as if she'd done something wrong by not helping out as her parents had wanted her to. Maybe Carli was right, and she was being really selfish by not mucking in with her family. But all she'd done was stick her neck out for something she *really* wanted to do. Was that so wrong?

It was only when she was in bed that night that the guilty feelings started to pass away, as she remembered all the nice things about the day. She'd fed the dogs, which was fun, even tempting Jake, the Yorkshire terrier who'd been off his food since he got there, to eat something. Then she'd cleaned out a couple of the kennels when two sets of owners had collected their dogs – it had been so lovely to see the happy dogs reunited with their families again! The cleaning out just meant a bit of mopping and changing the blankets – nothing too horrible. And then, all afternoon, she'd played with two kittens, then sat and talked soothingly to a nervous Siamese cat, until it had fallen asleep. And after all that, Gemma was ready to drop off herself!

Even though she was tired that night, Gemma found it difficult to get to sleep. She kept thinking about how worn-out her mum and dad looked, and the guilty feeling crept back into her. Trust Lucy to play up, too! If she'd been nice, it wouldn't have been half so bad. Gemma cuddled her pillow thoughtfully. Well, next Saturday she'd just work extra hard for her mum and dad – she'd show them she knew a thing or two about family loyalty, after all!

Chapter 5

For all Gemma's plans to be a model daughter, she didn't realise she was going to have to put them into action quite so soon. At half-seven the next morning, when by rights she should still have been fast asleep, there was her mum, yanking the curtains open in her bedroom, so that the bright sunshine fell in on Gemma's face.

"Ugh... what? What's happening?" she muttered.

"Work, that's what's happening," said her mum briskly. "Now – do you want an egg for breakfast, or just toast?"

Gemma stared at the clock on her bedside table, and then at Mrs Gordon's face. "Mum, it's Sunday. It's only half-past seven!" she said, not quite understanding what was happening.

"I know," Mrs Gordon said. "Your dad's opening up the arches to try and get a few more hours in on the cars. So, I'm sorry to say, you and Lucy will have to come with us – and *you'll* have to keep an eye on Lucy, while I help your dad."

"But Mum..." Gemma said, her nose wrinkling up in horror.

"Sorry – all hands on deck, today," was the brisk reply. "So, chop chop!"

Gemma pulled the quilt over her head as soon as her mum left the room. It was *Sunday*! She wanted to clean out Thumper and spend some time with him! She'd been so busy yesterday, she had only had a minute to pop in some carrot scrapings and give his nose a quick stroke. He was going to think she was abandoning him at this rate!

Grumbling to herself, Gemma got out of bed. As she splashed cold water on her face in the bathroom to try and wake herself up, she remembered her plans from the night before – how she was going to really make an effort to help out. It didn't seem quite so appealing first thing on a Sunday morning.

One look at Lucy across the breakfast table and she realised she had her work cut out for her. Lucy was looking tired and peevish, and Gemma's heart

sank at the thought of spending the day with her grumpy sister.

As she was pushing some cabbage into the rabbit hutches and giving Thumper a quick morning cuddle, Gemma suddenly remembered that Carli was supposed to be coming round to see Snowball. She had no way of letting her know she'd be out. Gemma tickled Snowball's nose with a bit of straw, while she wondered what to do. Perhaps she could stay here with Lucy, and wait in for Carli…

Mr Gordon wasn't having any of it! "I'm not leaving you two on your own in the house!" he said when she asked. "For one thing, it's against the law, and for another, I dread to think what you'd get up to!"

"But what about Carli?" persisted Gemma.

"You'll have to leave a note on the front door," Mr Gordon told her. "She knows where the arches are, doesn't she? If she's that keen to see you, I'm sure she'll make it."

Gemma fumed as she wrote out the note. That wasn't the point! Carli wanted to see Snowball, who *wouldn't* be at the arches! And it wasn't fair expecting Carli to wander about all over town just to find her! Why couldn't her dad be a bit more flexible about the whole thing?

As it turned out, Carli's appearance at the arches turned out to be a blessing in disguise.

Gemma and Lucy had been told to play quietly in the small office at the back of the arches and, for the whole morning, Lucy had wanted to do nothing but play with her Barbie dolls. Unfortunately for Gemma, *she* had to play along, too – dull, dull, dull!

Carli turned up after lunch with Annie in tow, their mum fussing behind them. The little girls were delighted to see each other. "Annie, come and play Barbies with me!" Lucy said at once. "Gemma's rubbish – she won't do proper voices, or anything!"

"I'm *so* sorry you've had to come all the way over here," Gemma said to Carli's mum.

"That's all right, Gemma, we had a nice walk, didn't we, girls?" replied Mrs Pike. Gemma smiled apologetically at Carli. "And I promise we'll be going back fairly soon, so we can play with the rabbits, then."

Carli shrugged. "No probs, Gems. Hey, you can get off, now, Mum, Mr Gordon will take us back." Carli hugged her mum goodbye and turned back to Gemma. “My Auntie Hayley and Uncle Gavin are coming down from Scotland later today,” she explained. “Mum wants us out of the way while she cleans the flat up. And if Annie and Lucy play together, that’s both our problems sorted at once!” She paused, and looked at Gemma’s gloomy face. “How come you’re all here anyway?”

“Mum said Lucy was a nightmare yesterday,” Gemma told her in a low voice, “so Dad’s behind with the work, and wants to catch up. I know it’s daft, but I really feel as if it’s all my fault. Is it so wrong to go for what you really want?”

Carli bit her lip. “That’s a tough one,” she said sympathetically. “But at least this is just one job for your dad – OK, so it’s a lot of work, and might last a few weeks, but at least it’ll come to an end. And then you can be at Paws every single Saturday for the rest of your life, if you want to!”

Gemma managed a smile. “You’re right – as usual,” she said. “And, hopefully, it’ll only be a few Saturdays and Sundays I’m here – and Paws was *so* worth it!” Her face lit up at the memory.

“I was wondering how long you’d keep quiet!” Carli joked. “Go on, then – tell me *everything*!”

After that, Sunday became a whole lot better. Carli was brilliant at drawing, and once Gemma had told her all about Paws, Carli whipped her drawing pad out and started sketching funny pictures of Lucy and Annie. Before long, the little girls were in stitches and thoroughly enjoying themselves.

The next day at school, the girls discussed their weekends over lunch. "*Namaste,*" Sunita greeted them, as they sat down. "*Tum kaisa ho*?"

"Eh?" said Lauren. "What are you on about?"

Sunita giggled. "Ahh, I'm learning to be a 'proper Indian girl', remember? That means, 'Hello, how are you?' And '*meira naam Sunita hai*' – that means, 'my name is Sunita'."

"We know your name's Sunita!" snorted Lauren. "We've known you for about five years now, Sunny!"

"So how was it?" Gemma asked. "Was it as deadly as you thought it was going to be?"

Sunita chewed a mouthful of sandwich, thoughtfully. "It was OK, I suppose," she said, "considering it was Saturday and I had to get up early for it. But Aunty Rita, my teacher, is all right, and it all seems quite easy. *And* I asked her all the

words for 'marriage', 'wife', and things like that. So, if Gran starts discussing Vikram and this Jamila again, I can find out if she really *is* talking about an arranged marriage!"

"Very sneaky!" said Carli, admiringly.

"Talking of old lover-boy," Lauren put in smugly, "I have some major gossip you may be interested in..." She paused teasingly, and raised her eyebrows at the other three.

Gemma nearly choked on her cheese sandwich at the look on her friend's face. "What? What is it?"

"Get this... Guess who I saw holding hands and giggling outside the paper shop yesterday? Yes, Vikram Banerjee and... Tracie Kelly! They were looking very cosy, too! Your gran's going to have to move fast, Sunita. I don't reckon Tracie's her idea of the perfect blushing bride!"

Gemma and Carli started giggling and making kiss-y noises, but Sunita looked shocked and stared at Lauren as if she couldn't believe her ears. "Are you sure?" she said finally. "Are you sure it was Vikram?"

"It was him, all right!" Lauren said, nodding. "No doubt about it!"

"But..." Sunita was so taken aback, she could hardly speak. "But... he shouldn't be doing that! If my parents saw him – or someone else saw him and told them – he'd be in big trouble. I mean, *big*!"

Gemma and Carli stopped giggling abruptly, once they saw how serious Sunita was. "They wouldn't approve, I take it?" Gemma said.

"Too right, they wouldn't!" Sunita said. "Especially if they've got plans for him and this Jamila girl – it'll be the last thing they want!"

Lauren crunched her mouthful of crisps thoughtfully. "I know what we should do," she said. "We should follow him one night, to see what he's up to!"

"Yeah!" said Sunita, eagerly. "Just so I can check it all out myself." She grinned suddenly as an idea occurred to her. "And then I'll threaten to tell Mum and Dad about what he's been up to and he'll have to be *very* nice to me for a while..."

"I'm sure he'd want to do some chores for you, once he found out that you knew!" said Carli.

"Maybe just the washing-up, hoovering, tidying your bedroom, preparing little snacks for you..." added Gemma.

"It's a brilliant idea!" Sunita smiled. "We'll have to let Anya know, too. How about Wednesday?"

"Fine with me," Lauren said, and Carli nodded, too.

"Oh – you'd better count me out," said Gemma,

apologetically. "Mum's allowed me to pop into Paws after school as I'm missing Saturday."

Lauren raised an eyebrow. "I'm impressed," she said. "How did you manage to get that past your dad?"

Gemma grinned. "By working on my mum! Carli and I did such a good job keeping Lucy quiet, she said she'll let me go straight after school on Wednesday."

"Cool!" said Carli.

"I'm only allowed to help Sheena with the evening feed and a couple of walks before I've got to go straight back home," Gemma added. "But it's better than nothing!"

"What about Tuesday, then?" Sunita tried.

"Tuesday's fine with me," Lauren said.

"Me too," said Carli. "Gems?"

"Er... I actually promised I'd walk Nelson, you know, Mrs Crick's dog, that day. Sorry... I'm trying to get in Mum's good books."

"Gemma Gordon, you're animal mad!" scolded Lauren. "We're never going to see you at this rate, if you're scrubbing out smelly dog kennels or walking that mangy old Nelson every night!"

"Mmm, it must be lovely working at Paws," agreed Sunita. "Washing out those gross feeding bowls..."

Gemma laughed. "I haven't been asked to do that yet," she said. "But even if I am, I won't mind! It's just so great, there, I –"

"Here we go, you lot," warned Lauren. "Why I adore Paws Kennels, by Gemma Gordon. A true story of one girl's undying *lurrve*!"

"No, honestly, it's brilliant!" Gemma protested, laughing. "Best thing I've ever done in my life! My big chance!"

"Just as long as you don't forget your best friends, that's all," said Lauren. "Or maybe you don't want to be part of the gang any more, if you're too busy for us these days?"

She knew it was only a joke, but Gemma felt so horrified at the thought that she immediately put her little finger out. "No way!" she said. "Never!"

The others linked little fingers and murmured their secret oath.

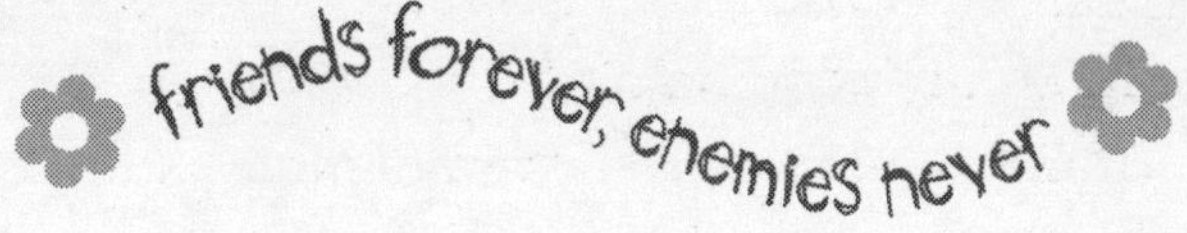

"That's better," grinned Lauren. "I was starting to think I was going to have to grow a tail for a minute! Woof, woof!"

"Ha, ha!" said Gemma. "Well, you'll have to lead the mission without me, this time – but I

promise I'll be at the next one!"

"Next one?" yelped Sunita. "How many girlfriends has Vikram got?" She pretended to think. "OK, you're let off just this once," she said. "I don't want to be second-best to a dribbling spaniel, either!" She turned to Lauren and Carli. "Shall we say Wednesday, then?"

"Sounds good to me," said Carli.

"Excellent!" said Sunita, all business-like. "And then we'll find out just what my sneaky big brother's up to!"

Chapter 6

On Wednesday evening, Gemma went off to the kennels, while Carli, Lauren and Sunita met up with Anya outside the row of shops near Duston Middle School. This was where Vikram had been spotted before by Lauren, and, as Anya pointed out, wrong-doers always returned to the scene of the crime!

Anya, as usual, had dressed up specially for the occasion. She had on a trendy pair of combat trousers – "to look the part" – a dark top – "easier to hide in the shadows" – and some Nikes – "so that we can run away if he gets cross and starts chasing us!"

"I thought I'd put my best tracksuit on, too," Lauren teased. "A detective has to look good, after all!"

"Where do we start, then?" Carli said.

"It's seventeen hundred hours: no sign of the suspect," Anya whispered dramatically, and the others giggled.

"Anya, we're not in a war film, you know!" spluttered Sunita.

Anya sighed crossly. "If you're going to do something, you might as well do it properly!" she snapped. "I read somewhere that – "

"Ooh, ooh, sighting of suspect!" gabbled Carli excitedly, gesturing across the road.

"Sighting confirmed!" agreed Lauren, clutching at Sunita's arm. "Suspect is alone on opposite side of road. Quick – look inconspicuous! Sunny, hide!"

Sunita ducked behind the newsagent's bin obediently. "Ugh, it stinks down here!" she moaned.

Lauren, Carli and Anya huddled together, trying to look as invisible as possible, so that if Vikram happened to glance across the road, all he would have seen was their three backs.

After a few seconds, Anya sneaked a peek across the road. "Danger over!" she hissed. "Suspect has now moved out of range!"

"Out of range?" snorted Sunita. "What were you planning to do, *shoot* him?" She got to her feet, and the four girls peered round the corner, craning

their necks to see where Vikram had got to.

"There he is!" Sharp-eyed Lauren pointed him out. "Suspect now approaching traffic lights. Follow that boy!"

Gemma, meanwhile, was helping Sheena with the feeds. The dogs got theirs first because they were the noisiest, and the sooner they settled down, the better! Gemma got the fourteen feeding bowls out of the cupboard and lined them up on the kitchen counter. That was the easy part – the difficult bit was remembering what to feed each dog!

"The two collies get fresh meat every night," Sheila said. "Lucky devils, their owners insist on it! It's in the pan on the cooker – should be cool by now."

Gemma started to chop it up as Sheena continued. "Archie – the Jack Russell – needs vitamin tablets before every meal. They're up on the shelf there, see? He's quite good about taking them now."

Sheena started to pour a saucer of milk. "Oh, are you going to feed the cats now, as well?" Gemma asked.

"No, this is for Poochie, the Spaniel in kennel

10. He likes milk every evening with his food – he's used to sharing with a cat at home," Sheena explained.

It was all a bit complicated, but Gemma enjoyed taking the bowls of food and water around to the hungry dogs, who were all *very* pleased to see her! "Here you go – hey, calm down!" she laughed, as the barking got even louder. "Don't worry, it's coming!"

Then it was the cats' turn. One very spoilt Persian cat was given boiled chicken every other day, the kittens needed special food for their young stomachs and one fat, black cat had a saucer of evaporated milk with a few drops of warm water in it every night.

"How do you remember it all?" Gemma wondered aloud.

"Oh, I don't!" Sheena laughed, and pointed to a large wipe-off wall-chart which gave details of every pet staying there, including likes, dislikes, special needs, owners' contact numbers and date to be picked up. "That's what runs this place – that chart. I'd be lost without it!"

The whole feeding operation took about half an hour in all, and then Gemma took Archie and one of the terriers out for a walk. She had to admit, she wasn't too sorry she wasn't allowed out alone with the bigger dogs – she could imagine herself being dragged all over town!

The other four girls *were* being dragged all over town, however, by Vikram.

"Where on earth is he going?" grumbled Lauren.

First of all, they'd trailed him down the road and past the school. Then he'd turned off to the left, climbed over a fence and gone down a long muddy path to the school playing fields, before pushing through a thick hedge to get to the woods on the other side.

The girls had hung about in the shadows, sneaking along in single file, until they got to the hedge.

"Do we follow?" Carli said, frowning at the tall, bushy obstacle in front of them. It was impossible to see just where Vikram had got through it – the brambles looked strong and forbidding from where the girls were standing, with no visible way through.

Anya scowled in the evening light. "It's going to ruin my clothes – look at the state my Nikes are in already!" Following Vikram along the streets and past the school had been exciting, but climbing over that fence had been awful and *now* they were in a muddy field… *Ugh*! All she wanted to do was go home, lie on her nice, comfortable sofa and watch telly.

The others exchanged glances. "What do you say, Sunita?" Lauren asked. "He's *your* brother, after all. It's up to you."

Sunita thought about it. "I really want to find out what's going on," she admitted after a moment. "The more I hear from Gran, the more I think she's planning this marriage. Last night I heard her on the phone again, and she said *bibi* which means 'wife', and mentioned Jamila and Vikram again. I mean, something's *definitely* going on. I've *got* to suss out what Vik's up to."

"OK, on we go," said Lauren, sticking her head and arms into the hedge, and scrambling through.

Anya sighed, but gamely tried forcing her own head through. "Ow!" she cried, as a twig snapped in her hair and a thorn scratched her hand.

"Push yourself forward," called Lauren encouragingly. "The harder you push, the quicker you get through!"

Anya tried a big shove off her back foot, but found herself now totally trapped in the hedge. "Help!" she called in a muffled voice. "I think I'm

– *ow*! – stuck!"

Carli and Sunita clutched each other with silent laughter, trying not to erupt into giggles at the sight of Anya's combat-trousered bottom sticking out of the bushes.

"I mean it!" yelled Anya, crossly. "I can't move! Will somebody *please* help me?"

Lauren reached through and grabbed her hand. "Come on, you loser," she said, tugging at her friend. "Push out with your elbows as if you're swimming! That's it! Now – *heave*!"

With one big yank from Lauren and a hard push from Sunita on the other side, Anya finally struggled through the hedge and fell sprawling on to the grass. She picked herself up, crossly, and wiped her clothes down. Great, now some threads had pulled in her top because of that stupid hedge. This was getting worse by the minute!

Sunita was about to clamber through next, but on the other side, Anya was looking all around. "So where is he?" she demanded. "Where's that stupid boy gone, now?"

Lauren looked around, guiltily. Their suspect was nowhere to be seen.

Sunita scrambled through with a crash, landing at their feet.

"Er, Sunny..." Lauren said hesitantly. "We

appear to have lost your brother..."

"Carli, don't bother coming through," Anya called bitterly. "There's no point. Vikram's given us the slip."

"What on earth do you think he was doing down here, anyway?" wondered Sunita. "I mean, I've heard of secret meetings between couples, but this is ridiculous! I can't see Tracie Kelly acting like a commando, scrambling over fences and through bushes, just to snog my brother!"

"Yeah, and like she could walk five steps in those heels she wears, anyway," said Anya.

Lauren groaned suddenly, and smacked her forehead. "Don't you see?" she exclaimed. "We've played right into his hands! He must have *known* we were following him and he's led us on a wild goosechase into the middle of nowhere!"

"And now he's probably laughing his head off, as he goes to meet Tracie somewhere completely different!" said Anya, scowling at the thought of having to clamber back through that awful hedge again. "I'm going off your brother, Sunita – in a *big* way!"

"Ready to go, Gemma?"

"Dad!" Gemma couldn't believe how quickly the time had gone. It felt like she'd only just arrived!

Reluctantly, she said goodbye to Poochie, the spaniel she'd been grooming, and went into the house to find her jacket and to say thank you to Sheena.

When Gemma came out of the front door, she saw Dad talking to Matt Jamison outside the surgery.

"Ah, here she is," said Matt with a wink. "I was just telling your dad, I've been hearing great things about you from Sheena. She says you're wonderful with the animals!"

Gemma's eyes shone with happiness. "*Really?*" she asked.

Matt nodded. "Really. Is that what you'd like to do when you're older, do you think? Work with animals?"

"Oh, yes," said Gemma. "I love animals. I'd really like to..." She hesitated, feeling embarrassed in front of him. "One day, I'd really like to do what *you* do – be a vet."

Matt laughed. "Well, good for you," he said. "You'll have to pop in and see us next door, one day. I could show you what goes on behind the scenes at the surgery, if you want."

Gemma's jaw dropped. "Could I?" she asked excitedly. "Could I, *really?*"

"Of course!" Matt said. "Sheena's told me that you're very gentle and patient with her lot, and that's just the sort of person who makes a good vet. Animals get frightened when they're ill, the same as we do, so they need calm, kind people around them. If you carry on the way you're doing, you'll be great!"

Mr Gordon cleared his throat to interrupt them. "Well, anyway, let's get you back, Gems. Your tea will be ready," he said gruffly. "See you soon, Matt. Come on, love, in the car."

Gemma put her seatbelt on, her fingers shaking with pride at what Matt had said to her. "Did you hear him, Dad?" she gabbled excitedly. "He said I'd make a good vet! Isn't that *brilliant*?"

"Mmm," said Mr Gordon, looking straight ahead at the road. "Very nice. But just you remember, there'll be plenty of time for all that when you're a bit older. We let you come here tonight as a special one-off, so don't go getting

ahead of yourself, all right? There're more important things to think about right now!"

Gemma sighed as her excitement started trickling away. OK, she *knew* what her dad was getting at! Did he have to remind her of it every five minutes? Did he have to be such a wet blanket *all* the time?

Chapter 7

Over in the Pike household, it seemed that no sooner had Aunt Hayley and Uncle Gavin gone back to Scotland, than Carli's Aunty Michelle arrived on Saturday morning.

"Yoo-hoo!" her voice boomed around the kitchen.

Carli, who'd been sketching in her bedroom, put her book away and suddenly remembered the promise she'd made to Anya about a shopping trip. Carli knew Anya still hadn't had a chance to buy the trousers she was so keen to get, and she also knew Aunty Michelle would be on for a shopping spree at the drop of a hat.

Despite all that, Carli felt a bit reluctant to arrange it. For one thing, she was still slightly wary of Anya. She hadn't known her as long as the other girls had and, because they went to different schools, she and Anya hadn't really had time to get to know each other properly. There was something else, too... Although Carli hated to admit it, Aunty Michelle might be a problem in herself. Michelle was one of those people who was always great fun – loud, jolly and enthusiastic – but Carli was pretty sure that Anya might look down her nose at her aunt. She was a million miles away from Anya's own family.

"So I said, look, darling, I don't care if your name's Leonardo diCaprio, you're not coming in this house!"

Carli heard her mum and aunt shrieking with laughter in the kitchen at Michelle's latest outrageous story, and tried to picture Sacha Michaels, Anya's sophisticated mother, laughing in quite the same way. Impossible!

Still, looking on the bright side, Carli told herself, this could be a good chance to get to know Anya better. With Sunita at a Hindi lesson, Gemma minding Lucy, and Lauren going to swimming training, it would just be the two of them. Anya was very pretty and confident, the kind of person Carli wished she was more like. And if Gemma, Lauren and Sunita liked her so much, she *must* be OK...

Carli's mind was made up and she went into the

kitchen, still in her stripy pyjamas.

"Hello, sweetie!" Michelle cried as she walked in, and swooped down on Carli for a big hug. "Ooh, nice p-j's, Carli – stripes are very 'in' this season, you know? You're a trend-setting young thing, what are you?"

Carli blushed and giggled. Aunty Michelle really was a bit bonkers sometimes. Oh, she hoped Anya liked her!

"How are you?" she asked, helping herself to a bowl of cereal.

"Oh, only madly in love with a gorgeous man from Northborough!" exclaimed Michelle.

Mrs Pike snorted. "I didn't know there *was* such a thing," she said.

"Well, I've gone and snapped up the only one, then," Michelle said, grinning wickedly. "Naughty old me, eh! He's worth it, though, Suze – you should see him! Six foot two inches of sheer hunkiness! And his eyes... Oh! Every time I look into them, it's like drowning!"

"You'll have to borrow Annie's armbands next time you see him, then, won't you?" sniffed Mrs Pike. Although she sounded disapproving, Carli knew she secretly loved hearing what her wild younger sister got up to. "So what's his name, then?"

"Wayne," said Michelle, and pulled a face. "Not very romantic, I know. But you can forgive some things, can't you? Especially with a bum like his... Ooops! Sorry, Carli, I forgot you were in the room!"

Carli went red again, but smiled at her aunt. "That's OK," she said. She paused a moment, wondering whether or not to ask about a shopping trip. If Aunty Michelle was in such a wild mood, it might not be such a good idea. Still, what else would she do? Carli figured she might as well go for it. "Aunt Michelle, do you have any plans today?"

"Apart from gossiping with your mum about my gorgeous Wayne, not really, no," Michelle replied. "Why, got anything in mind?"

Carli explained the situation, about how Anya desperately wanted to buy some new trousers. Michelle immediately looked sympathetic. A dedicated shopper herself, she understood Anya's problem all too well.

"Oh, of course!" she said. "A good shopping trip is definitely in order! Fancy it, Suze?"

Mrs Pike looked apologetic. "After a week of relatives staying, I feel like collapsing on the sofa in front of a good film, to be honest," she said. "Annie's going to one of her friend's birthday parties this afternoon, so it would be wonderful to have the flat to myself for a bit..."

"Absolutely!" said Michelle firmly. "You put your feet up, while we get on our shopping shoes!" She rummaged in her large silver handbag before finally fishing out a pink mobile phone. "Want to give this Anya a call?" she said. "Let's arrange to meet about eleven, yeah?"

Anya had completely forgotten about Carli's vague offer the other week, so was caught off guard when the phone rang.

"Oh, hello," she said. "What am I up to? Not much, why?"

As Carli explained that she and her aunt would be in town if Anya wanted to join them, Anya felt like biting off her own tongue. She really didn't want to hang out with this barmy-sounding aunt of Carli's all day! 'Quick!' she told herself. 'Think of an excuse!'

"Er... Yeah, fine," Anya found herself saying, as her brain refused to co-operate. Oh no! Why had she said that? "Er... Where do you want to meet?"

They arranged a time and place, and Anya pulled a sick face as she put the phone down.

Meeting outside C&A! Things weren't looking good.

Over at the arches, Gemma wasn't having a good day either. She was trying to keep Lucy quiet by drawing pictures, like Carli had done the Sunday before, but her little sister wasn't interested in the slightest.

"I'm bored with this horrible office," she kept whining. "And it stinks! Why can't we play outside?"

"Because Dad wants us to stay in here," Gemma said, for about the twentieth time. "I know, why don't we play hangman?"

"Because it's boring!" Lucy whinged. "Why can't we play outside?"

"I just told you why not!" Gemma yelled, getting sick of that question. Sick of Lucy, too, and sick of the arches. And to think, she could have been at Paws today! Life just wasn't *fair*!

"Girls, what's all that shouting?" called Mrs Gordon. "Can you play nicely, please? I don't want to have to come in there!"

Lucy stuck her tongue out at Gemma.

Gemma stuck hers out in reply. Why was this day going so slowly?

Anya was ten minutes late to meet Carli and her aunt in town. For one thing, she hadn't been able to decide what to wear, and for another, she didn't want anyone from school to see her hanging around outside C&A. That would instantly lose her some cool points!

Anya thanked her mum for dropping her off, then spotted Carli. She was standing with a woman who *had* to be her aunt.

"Ah, hello, Anya," said Michelle. "Heard you needed some trousers. Not to worry! We'll sort you out, won't we, Carli?"

Carli smiled nervously. She could see Anya's eyes bulging slightly with surprise at her aunt's outfit. She was used to the way Michelle dressed by now, but she supposed that a fake fur zebra-print jacket, thigh-high boots and a pink mini-dress was a slightly unusual outfit for a Saturday afternoon shopping in town.

"Now then," Michelle was saying, bustling them along. "I know a great boutique we can try for trousers, Anya, but I just want to pop into Oxfam first – see what bargains they've got today."

Carli caught sight of the beginnings of a sneer on Anya's face. Oh dear, this wasn't a very good start. Anya had probably never been near a charity shop in her life!

Inside Oxfam, Aunty Michelle was a woman possessed. She skimmed through the racks of clothes with a practised air, pulling out anything that looked wild or garish as she went. "Come on, let's try this lot on for a laugh," she said, when a huge pile of clothes had been gathered. "Me and Wayne are going to a Seventies night next weekend – got to look the part!"

"I'm not sure..." Anya said, sounding a bit haughty. The thought of wearing someone else's clothes made her feel sick!

"Oh, don't be shy," breezed Michelle, misreading Anya's reply completely. "I'll go first!"

She bustled into the changing room while the two girls waited outside. Anya looked out of the window. This was a terrible mistake! She should never have agreed to come!

Next thing she knew, there was a loud "Ta-da!", and the girls looked round to see Michelle flouncing about in a yellow and turquoise patterned mini-dress, silver platform boots, pink feather boa and, to top it off, a bright red Afro wig on her head.

Carli couldn't help but burst out laughing at the sight of her aunt shimmying around the shop

looking like she'd just stepped out of a time-warp. Then, to her surprise, she heard Anya giggling as well. Red in the face, the two clutched at each other in hysterics, as Michelle stood in the shop window, wiggling her bottom at all the shoppers in the High Street. "What do you think, girls? Is it me?"

"Yes, definitely," Carli spluttered. "Do you think Wayne will like it?"

"Oh, he'll love it!" Michelle said firmly. "Now then – it's time you two had a go. Anya – how about these gold hot-pants? They look about your size! And Carli, there are some lovely lime-green flares here for you to try on..."

Before long, the three of them were weak with laughter, as they tried on more and more crazy outfits. Anya forgot all her thoughts about 'charity clothes' and was soon having the time of her life, prancing about in hot-pants and some red fluffy mules that Carli's aunt insisted were 'totally her'. Even the shop assistants enjoyed the show, especially when Michelle bought a couple of things for her night out with Wayne.

"It's a shame to leave this wig behind," she said regretfully, putting it back on the shelf, "but you can't have everything, I suppose..."

"Oh, buy it," Anya said, as if she and Aunt

Michelle were old mates. "It looked great with that outfit!"

"Do you think so?" Michelle asked, looking pleased. "Oh, go on, then! You've talked me into it!"

Carli realised she was really enjoying herself as they left Oxfam. Anya and Michelle were chattering away about their favourite clothes shops in town. OK, so Carli'd never heard of most of them – she was just relieved that Anya was having a good time. She found herself smiling at the pair of them, nattering away. They were a bit of an odd couple, really – Anya in her trendy designer gear, and Michelle looking like she'd just stepped out of the Seventies in all her charity shop bargains!

The three of them dedicated a good hour to buying the right pair of trousers for Anya.

"Your aunt is amazing!" Anya confided to Carli, as Michelle went off to hunt down yet another pair to try on. "I wish I had an aunt like her – you're *so* lucky!"

Carli glowed with pride and pleasure. Anya Michaels telling *her*, Carli Pike, she was lucky!

"I've got the perfect ones!" Michelle announced as she came back, brandishing a pair of black velvet bootleg trousers. "Velvet to keep you warm at the ice-rink – and very trendy right now, too!

Bootleg, like you wanted, Anya. Try them on!"

Even Carli could see that the trousers looked great on Anya, and they were immediately snatched up and paid for. Anya was delighted.

"Now then," Michelle said, as they left the shop. "I think we need a break after such a hardcore shopping session. Knickerbocker Glory, anyone? My treat!"

Anya linked arms with Carli on one side, and Michelle on the other. "This is my idea of heaven," she said, beaming at the two of them. "What a brilliant day I'm having! Thank you, both of you!"

"Oh, not at all! My pleasure!" Michelle said, smiling back.

Carli squeezed Anya's arm in hers. "I'm enjoying it, too," she said, a grin spreading all over her face. Everything was better with a friend!

Chapter 8

Although Carli and Anya had had a fantastic time out on Saturday, Lauren hadn't particularly enjoyed her swimming practice. Peter, the coach, was in a bad mood for some reason, and had shouted at Lauren that she wasn't trying hard enough in one of her races.

"That was a bit half-hearted, wasn't it?" he'd said, as she reached the end of the pool, panting and spluttering. That stung – Lauren prided herself on always throwing every ounce of energy behind every sporting thing she did: football, swimming, netball, running – she'd always give one hundred per cent!

Lauren tried telling herself that Peter was just being grouchy and to forget it, but the stubborn side of her kept thinking about it, and getting

cross. As a result, she'd been overdoing it ever since: on Sunday she dragged her older brother, Ben, and some of his mates out for a kick-about in the park, then had an energetic game of swingball in the back garden for hours with Gemma. On Monday, it was footy practice and she made sure she ran like a hare for every ball – so much so, that she scored three of their team's winning four goals. Not bad – but not good enough for Lauren. She'd show Peter she never did anything by halves! She was determined to be in top shape for next week's swimming.

On Tuesday, she went for a run with her dad. As Mr Standish worked at the sports centre, he was pretty fit himself, so she had a good old work-out just keeping up with him!

On Wednesday, Lauren was just about to go for a quick run around the park again, when Bart, the Standishes' family dog, spotted her putting her trainers on. Immediately, he started jumping up and down, barking excitedly.

"No, I'm not taking you out," Lauren laughed, as he pushed his wet brown nose under her arm hopefully and woofed again. "Hey, calm down!"

Bart started licking her face. Then, he put his big paws on her and barked again.

"Oh, all right, all right," Lauren said, unable to

resist those big brown eyes. "Let's do it, Bart! Let's go walkies!"

As soon as she said that, Bart bounded about barking louder than ever. He was a medium-sized scruffy golden mongrel and had more energy than a generator. He was only two, so still had lots of puppyish ways. And walks were pretty much Bart's favourite thing – lots of sniffing around, running, noisy barking, playing fetch and generally having a wonderful time!

"Come on, then," Lauren said, giggling as she clipped his lead on. "Take me for a run, you big baby."

She knocked on the Gordons' door as she went past, in case Gemma fancied joining her. She knew Gemma loved Bart almost as much as the Standishes did. "Gems around?" she asked Mrs Gordon who answered the door.

Mary Gordon smiled at tomboy Lauren. "She's at Paws again, love," she said. "I think she's arranged to have a look around the vet's surgery this evening. You know Gemma – couldn't resist!"

"I bet," Lauren said, grinning. "Hey, that's brilliant though, isn't it? She must be chuffed to bits!"

Bart started jumping around impatiently. "I'd better go," Lauren said. "Bart's taking me for a run

– thinks he's fitter than I am!"

"You show him, Lauren!" said Mrs Gordon. "No one can beat you!"

Lauren and Bart set off. First stop, the park, where Bart could be let off the lead and have a mad half-hour, chasing sticks and imaginary squirrels, barking at other dogs and having a whale of a time. Dog heaven, thought Lauren with a smile, as he bounced back and forth, half a branch hanging out of his mouth, grinning a big doggy grin at her.

It was thirsty work though, chasing about with a manic mongrel, so after a while Lauren felt a craving for a drink. Luckily, the sports centre where her dad worked wasn't too far from the park, so she decided to head that way and get a can from one of the machines in the foyer.

Lauren whistled for Bart, clipped on his lead and started making for the exit. "Sorry, matey," she told him as he trotted behind her. "If I don't get a drink soon, I'll conk out, and that won't do, will it?"

Lauren and Bart were just getting close to the sports centre, when Lauren suddenly spotted a couple sitting on the wall outside the main reception area. They were kissing as if they were trying to beat a world record! Lauren's eyebrows leapt almost to her hairline in surprise. There was

Vikram again, with that Tracie Kelly! So he *was* seeing her!

Just for a second, Lauren had a funny feeling inside, almost as if she was jealous or something. What did he see in her? Tracie Kelly had horsy teeth and knew *nothing* about sport! *And* she had spots, Lauren had noticed. Big red ones, on her chin. Ugh!

Lauren tossed her blonde ponytail, feeling a bit put out. Well, Vikram obviously liked the girl, the way he was kissing her. Last time she'd seen them together, they'd only been holding hands and Lauren had thought that maybe it wasn't that serious between them – obviously it was now!

Suddenly Lauren came to her senses. She had to tell Sunita! Sunny had been so worried about the pair of them getting caught – and look where they were! Almost on the Duston Road, outside the sports centre where people were coming and going all the time! Gossip spread like wildfire in Northborough, her mum always said...

Lauren looked around, not wanting Vikram to see her. Aha! There was a phone box the other side of the road – that would do! Together, she and Bart ran towards the busy Duston Road. Lauren came to a stop at the kerb, but excited Bart thought this was a bit more exercise and carried on running.

Lauren was in such a daze, she wasn't paying attention to him and felt the lead slip out of her hand as Bart charged away.

"Bart!" she yelled, then watched in horror as he bounded out into the traffic. A car whizzed past him, blaring its horn. "Bart!" she screamed again, terrified of what was going to happen.

Bart heard her, but was too freaked out by the noisy traffic to know what to do. He charged further across the road and Lauren screamed again, as a car skidded to a halt in front of him, brakes squealing, horn blaring.

The cars had all stopped and Lauren stared in horror at the still, brown body that was lying in the road.

"No!" she screeched, and raced over. The driver got out of his car, and went over to join her.

"I'm *so* sorry," he was saying, though Lauren couldn't take in the words. "He just rushed out in front of me! There was nothing I could do!"

Lauren burst into tears and pressed her face against Bart's body as gently as she dared. He gave a faint whimpering sound and she felt his heart beating. He was alive! She couldn't believe it!

"You should get him to a vet," the man was saying. "Do you want me to give you a lift?"

Even though Lauren wanted to say yes, she

knew she shouldn't get into a car with anyone, even if this man did seem nice. "No, thank you," she said, tears still pouring down her face. "My dad works over there. He'll take me. But could you please, please do me a massive favour, and get him for me? I can't leave my dog on his own! Ask for Mr Standish – tell him it's an emergency!"

Sobbing and sniffing loudly, Lauren helped the man pick Bart up very carefully and put him down on the pavement.

Lauren wiped her nose on her sleeve, and tried to pull herself together. Right. This was important. Bart might die any second. She had to put him first!

Quickly, she took off her sports jacket and wrapped up Bart to keep him warm. One of his legs was bleeding, and it was hanging at a funny angle, as if it was broken. "Oh, Bart," she whispered. "Please don't die! *Please*... don't die!"

It seemed like ages before Mr Standish roared up beside her in his car. He jumped out of the driver's side and raced around to see Bart.

"Up you come, boy," he said to the poorly dog and lifted him into the back seat, tucking him up in the old blanket that was always there. "In you get, Lauren. We'll go straight to the vet's."

"It's all my fault," Lauren blubbed. "I wasn't watching him properly, he just ran straight out, and the lead –"

"Let's just get round to the vet's and see what he's got to say about it," said Mr Standish practically. "We can talk about all that later."

Lauren sat in the back with Bart, cuddling him and whispering comforting things, even though he didn't seem to hear a word. She knew she could never forgive herself if anything happened to her beloved Bart – it was just too, too awful to even think about!

It was a busy evening at the vet's, and Matt Jamison was seeing to a budgie in the surgery.

The budgie hadn't been eating, the old lady who owned him said, and she was worried that something was wrong with him.

Matt was just about to give his opinion, when Gemma, his 'assistant for the evening' as he'd grandly called her, heard a familiar voice from the waiting room.

"Please! Can you help? My dog's been hit by a

car, and he's really badly hurt!"

Lauren? Lauren!

"Excuse me," Gemma muttered urgently and raced into the waiting-room.

"What are *you* doing here?" Lauren cried when she saw her. In the shock of Bart's accident, Lauren had forgotten all about Gemma being there. Gemma couldn't believe her eyes, seeing her best friend there with Mr Standish, and...

"Bart!" cried Gemma. "Oh, what happened?"

As soon as Lauren saw the concern on Gemma's face, she broke down in tears again. "It was all my fault," she wailed. "I should have been looking after him! And now he's going to die, all because of me!"

Gemma shut her eyes. She loved Bart, saw him every day of her life. She wanted to burst into tears, too, but she knew that crying wouldn't help Lauren one bit. Instead, she tried to stay calm. "You're in the best place now, Lauren," she said comfortingly. "The vet will help Bart, don't worry. I'll go and get him for you."

She didn't need to – Matt had already heard the noise and had come to see what was happening. "Pass him to me," he instructed Mr Standish. "That's it. I'll just take a quick look at – what did you say his name was? Bart? OK. Er, Mrs Wilson?"

he called to the old lady with the budgie. "I'm terribly sorry, would you mind going back to the waiting-room for a minute or two? Bit of an emergency, I'm afraid..."

Gemma squeezed Lauren's hand. "Try not to worry," she whispered, as they followed Matt into the treatment room.

There was a silence while Matt examined poor Bart. Lauren bit her lip so hard she thought it was going to bleed – she just couldn't bear waiting to hear how badly he'd been hurt! Every time she thought about how it had all happened so quickly, another tear rolled down her cheek.

Matt broke the silence after a few minutes. "Well, it's quite serious – but I'm pretty sure he'll be able to pull through without any lasting damage," he began. "He's got concussion – that means he's been knocked out – and has broken this front leg. Plus, it looks like there's some internal bleeding. That's the bad news. The good news is that he's a young dog, so he's fit and strong with good bones that will heal fairly easily. *And* the break in his leg looks pretty clean, so it should mend well. The main thing that concerns me is the internal injuries. It's always a bit difficult to say how much damage there is from a first look, but he'll have to stay here while his leg mends, so I can get a better idea of how extensive the bleeding is."

Lauren burst into fresh howls, and Gemma put an arm around her. "Hey, come on," said Gemma encouragingly. "It could have been much worse. With a bit of luck, he's going to be fine! He's a toughie, your Bart – there's no way one stupid car's going to get the better of him!"

Lauren choked on a sob. "But he's going to be all scared when he wakes up in here! He won't know what's happening!" She turned to Mr Standish. "Dad, can we stay here a bit longer with him, just till he wakes up? I hate the thought of him not knowing where he is!"

Mr Standish looked at his watch. "We've really got to get back to your mum," he said. "She's going out and needs the car. And he might not come round for hours yet, right, doc?"

"It could be a while, Lauren," Matt said.

"I'll be here for another hour yet, Lauren," Gemma told her. "And if he comes round then, he'll know me, won't he? And I'll come round to yours as soon as I get back tonight."

"Would you?" asked Lauren, blowing her nose loudly.

"Course I will," said Gemma, giving her a hug.

It was only when Lauren and Mr Standish left that Gemma suddenly felt a bit trembly, as the massive shock of what had happened hit her.

"Are you OK?" said Matt, seeing her face.

Gemma found herself sniffing. "Just... you know," she said, gesturing at Bart, who was still lying unconscious on the table. "I've known him since he was a puppy, too; we live next door, so he's almost like my dog..."

Matt put a kind hand on her shoulder. "Well, you did very well tonight, then, Gemma," he told her. "Even better than I thought. You were really great with that friend of yours, you kept your head, and said all the right things. You helped her, even though you were feeling upset, too!" He smiled at her. "Can't do better than that, can you?"

Gemma smiled back, tearfully, feeling her spirits lift a bit. "Do you think so?" she said.

"Absolutely! Now, we need to see to Bart, and there's still the budgie to sort out. Let's get back to work!" He bent down to have a closer look at the dog, then looked back at Gemma. "You know, you're going to be a great vet!"

Chapter 9

With all the drama surrounding Bart's accident, Lauren had completely forgotten what had started it all off in the first place – her urgency to phone Sunita. When she and Mr Standish had got home, there had been more tears from Lauren and her mum, and howls from baby Harry, as she'd explained about how the accident had happened, and told everyone how sorry she was.

It was only later, when she was sitting in the bath trying to calm down, that she remembered why she'd been daydreaming in the first place. Of course – Vikram and Tracie! Sunita had to know!

Lauren stood up in the bath so fast that water slopped everywhere. She grabbed a towel, wrapped herself up in it and raced downstairs, dripping bubbles everywhere. "Mum, can I use the phone?

It's an emergency!" she said.

Mrs Standish looked at her daughter. "Another emergency?" she asked. "All right, then – as long as it's quick. And dry those bubbles off you before you drip on the carpet even more!"

Lauren dialled Sunita's number. "Sunita! I've got some major news for you," she said. "Repeat sighting of suspect with T.K. Yes, sure I'm sure!"

Anya was talking on the phone, too. At long last, Astrid had telephoned, offering the precious invite.

"Of course I'll come," said Anya, trying to sound as casual as possible. "When did you say it was again?" she added, knowing full well when the party was due to be held. It had been marked on her calendar ever since she'd heard about it, after all!

As she put the phone down, she couldn't help but give a triumphant cheer. Great! And she had those wicked black trousers to wear, as well! Perfect!

As Sunita put the phone down, she wasn't quite

ure what to make of Lauren's news. On the one and, she was concerned about her brother – but nore concerned about her parents finding out vhat he was up to. She had to warn him to be more secretive, otherwise someone was bound to ell Mr and Mrs Banerjee where their precious son ad been spending his evenings – and who he'd een with.

On the other hand, Sunita couldn't help but hink about all the ammunition this gave her. She ould really wind Vikram around her little finger y threatening to let the secret out to their mum nd dad. Hmmm... could be interesting!

Bart was still unconscious by the time Gemma left the vet's. Matt had taken a closer look at him now, and pointed out some nasty skin wounds to Gemma. Bart had obviously been dragged along the road by the force of the car and his side was quite badly torn up. Gemma shuddered. She wasn't usually squeamish, but it was pretty awful seeing an animal you loved in such a terrible state.

She heard her dad beeping his horn outside, and knew that her time was up. "Thank you so much for letting me look around," she said to

Matt, as she put on her coat.

"It's just a shame this had to happen, isn't it?" he said gently. "I hope it hasn't put you off being a vet. It's always the hardest bit, seeing a nasty injury like this – especially when it's actually an animal you know." He started walking out to the front door with her. "But you did very well back there, like I said. And I'll be ringing the Standishes with any news on Bart, so they'll be able to keep you up to date with how he is."

"Do you think... Would you mind... Would it be OK if I came in to see Bart after school tomorrow?" Gemma asked timidly. "I don't want you to think I'm hanging around, but he might want to see a familiar face – and I'm sure Lauren would want to see him, too..."

"Of course," said Matt, opening the front door and giving Mr Gordon a wave. "Absolutely. See you tomorrow, then!"

When Gemma and Lauren walked into the surgery the next day, Matt was busy with more pet patients, so a nurse took them round to a back room. Bart, still attached to a drip, was being kept in a large cage. As soon as he saw the girls, he gave a high-pitched bark and tried to stand up, but his bandaged leg was obviously so painful to stand on he fell back down again. He lay on a red blanket, panting and making small woofing noises.

"Oh, Bart!" exclaimed Lauren. "Hello, boy! What a *good* boy! How are you feeling?"

She stroked his nose through the bars, and Bart licked lovingly at her fingers. "How is he?" she asked the nurse. "What's happened to his leg? When did he come round?"

"The vet's put his leg in a cast," explained the nurse. "He X-rayed it last night, and it's quite a clean break, like he thought, so it'll mend in time. We'll have to leave the cast on for a few weeks though, I'm afraid, until the leg's strong enough for Bart to walk on again."

"What about inside?" asked Lauren nervously. "The vet said there was lots of bleeding."

"That's right," said the nurse. "So we've got to keep Bart here for a while, just to check that the bleeding doesn't go into his lungs. In any case, it'll take a bit of time for his insides to settle down after the accident."

"Oh, Bart, I'm so sorry," whispered Lauren. "I promise I'll never ever take my eyes off you again. Cross my heart and hope to die! I'm a stupid girl, aren't I, Bart? Not any more, though!" She stroked his nose gently. "Is he in a lot of pain?" she asked.

"He's OK," the nurse said. "He doesn't think much of the injections we've been giving him, but on the whole he's very good-tempered, considering what he's just been through."

"Oh, you *clever* boy!" Lauren said warmly. Then she looked at her watch. "Uh-oh – I'm going to be late for my football practice. Mind if I run on ahead, Gems?"

Gemma squeezed her arm. "Course not," she said. "See you tomorrow."

Gemma stayed a little while longer, talking to Bart and helping the nurse give him a pain-killing injection. She held him still, and Bart was so busy licking her hand, he didn't seem to notice the needle going in.

"Thank you," the nurse said, smiling. "You're Gemma, aren't you? Matt told me about you. I'm Lisa. Do feel free to pop in and see Bart whenever you want to."

"I wish I could," said Gemma. "But my mum and dad think I'm spending too much time here or at Paws as it is."

Lisa nodded, sympathetically. "That's a shame. It would really help Bart to feel better, seeing someone he knows about the place." A thought suddenly struck her. "Hey, Matt knows your dad, doesn't he? Why don't I ask Matt to persuade him it's a good idea for you to pop in more often? Just until Bart's better, anyway."

Gemma brightened. "Would you? That would be *so* cool!"

"'Course I would," smiled Lisa. "It's good for Bart, and I reckon it's good for you, too!"

Matt did a great job with Gemma's dad. Garry Gordon realised how poorly Bart was and allowed his daughter to pop into the vet's and the kennels' every day, even if only for half an hour before she went home for her tea.

Lauren came with her most days, and sometimes Carli and Sunita came as well, but as they were all busy with other things, it was usually Gemma who stuck around to help out Sheena wherever she could.

As Lisa had said, the dog was a good patient, but he seemed to be especially well-behaved whenever Gemma was there. He grew to hate his injections, and it was only really when Gemma was around to talk to him and comfort him that he would let Matt or Lisa give him the jab without a lot of fuss. Because of this, they'd taken to giving him any injections in the afternoons when Gemma was there to help out. Good old Bart, Gemma couldn't help thinking. In a way, he was really doing *her* a favour!

On the Thursday of that week, Gemma stopped by at the Standishes' house on her way home, after the usual visit to Bart. Lauren was hanging her swimming costume up on the washing line outside, so Gemma went straight out the back to find her.

"Been showing that Peter a thing or two?" she called up the garden.

Lauren turned round, smiling. "You know it!" she replied. "I knocked four seconds off my best time today, he was really pleased. Said I must have been working very hard – which of course, I have been!" She tossed her long wet hair back proudly. "But more important than any of that, what's the news on the Bart-front?" she asked. "How's he doing?"

"Really well," said Gemma. "He looks better and perkier every day, you know. And best of all, he'll only let the vet give him an injection when

I'm there! Honestly, I could kiss Bart, he makes me look *really* good in front of Matt!"

"Well, that's because you *are* so good with him, of course!" Lauren said, linking arms with Gemma as they started walking back to the house. "Honestly, Gems, you've been brilliant full stop. Just think, if you hadn't started helping out at Paws, you'd never have been there in the first place."

Gemma shrugged. "Well, you know, it's what I like doing..."

Lauren wasn't having any of this modesty. "Yeah, but Gems, the fact is, you've really put yourself out over Bart. I don't want to get all mushy on you, but you really helped me the night it all happened and you're really helping Bart, too. You're a true friend, Gemma Gordon, I mean it!"

Lauren held Gemma's little finger with her own, and together they mouthed their special phrase.

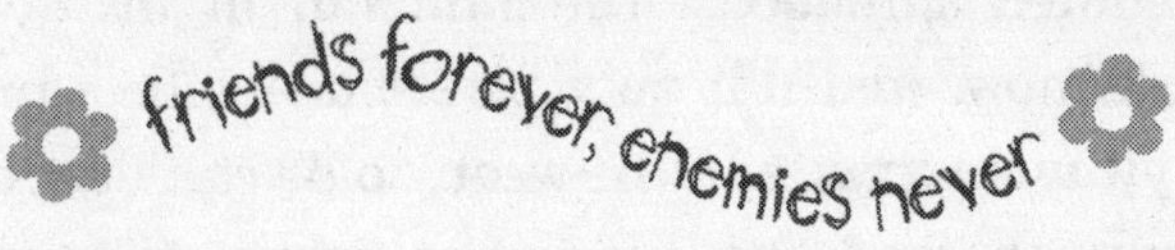

"I'm just glad to help Bart," Gemma started to say, but Lauren interrupted her.

"Hey – I've just had a thought... I've just had a *brilliant* thought!"

"Uh-oh," said Gemma. "What brilliant thought?"

"I've had an excellent idea about how I can say thanks to you properly." Lauren's eyes were shining. "What would you want most in the world?"

Gemma wasn't sure what her best friend was on about. "Oh, straight A's in tomorrow's maths test, everlasting chocolate cake in the fridge, longer summer holidays..."

"Yeah, and what else?"

"Well, you know – I'd love to be able to work at Paws every Saturday, with no more Lucy duty down the arches! But..."

"But nothing," Lauren said, impulsively. "Your wish is my command! I'll look after Lucy for you while your dad's got this job on, so you're free to go to Paws every Saturday!"

Gemma stared at her, as if she couldn't believe her ears. "*Really*? But what about swimming? Won't Peter flip if you miss practices?"

Lauren shrugged. "Let him! I'm in his good books now, and it'll only be for a a little while. Anyway, I go twice in the week, so he can't get too mad with me!" She grinned at Gemma's excited face. "Well? Is it a deal, or what?"

"It's a deal! Oh, Lauren, it's the best deal in the world!" cried Gemma, hugging her wonderful, generous friend.

"Great!" said Lauren. Then she spotted Mr Gordon over the fence. "Right – now to clear it with the boss," she whispered. "Hey, Mr Gordon!" she shouted over at him. "You've got a new helper down at the arches, on Saturdays!"

"Oh yeah?" came the reply. "And who might that be, then?"

"It's me!" Lauren beamed. "I'm going to do Lucy duty for a few weeks. Me and Gemma have sorted it all out!"

Mr Gordon folded his arms across his chest, and just for an awful moment, Gemma thought he was going to say no. "And what's brought this on?" he asked suspiciously. "More to the point – are you up to the job?"

"Oh, course I'm up to the job!" said Lauren easily. "Me and Lucy will be quiet as mice, don't you worry! And I'm doing it because your daughter's fab and I owe her one. That OK?"

For once in his life, Mr Gordon didn't quite know what to say. "Well, that's very good of you, Lauren," he managed in the end. He knew how bossy Lauren could be and was quite sure she would keep Lucy under strict control. "Let's hope Gemma appreciates what you're doing for her!"

"Oh, I do!" said Gemma quickly, and hugged Lauren again. "I do, I do, *I do*!"

Chapter 10

That evening, at the Banerjees', Sunita kept a close eye on her brother over dinner. Enough playing games, she'd decided she was going to confront him with the truth and see what he had to say for himself.

As soon as he'd finished eating, Vikram pushed his empty plate away. "Thanks," he said. "OK if I go out for a while?"

"Where are you going?" Sunita asked quickly.

"Out," was all he said. "Not that it's anything to do with you!"

Sunita heard her brother running upstairs – to get changed for Tracie, no doubt – and knew she had to act fast. As soon as he came downstairs again, she made her own excuses and went out into the hall, blocking the front door. Vikram came to a halt as he saw her standing there, arms firmly crossed over her chest, looking like she meant business!

"What's this?" he asked. "Come to apologise for being so nosey?"

"No way," she said.

"What, then? Because I'm in a hurry, if you don't mind." Vikram sounded as if he was losing his patience.

"Just wanted to let you know that I know where you're *really* going," Sunita snapped and, to Vikram's amazement, his little sister started making exaggerated kissing noises at him.

"What's up with you? Have you got something stuck in your teeth?" he asked sarcastically.

"Have *you* got something you should be telling Gran about?" Sunita countered, quick as a flash. "Something called *Tracie Kelly*, for example?!"

Vikram pulled a face and took another step forwards. "What's it to you, shorty? It's none of your business!" he said.

Sunita shrugged. She'd done her best to warn him! "Fine," she said. "Well, don't blame me when Mum and Dad find out and go ballistic..."

Vikram laughed, totally uninterested in his sister's threats. "Forget it, sis," he said. "I dumped her a couple of days ago. Easy come, easy go, you know me."

Sunita felt totally deflated. "Well, let's see what Jamila thinks of that," she said, as a last resort. "Your future wife!"

Vikram stared at her and suddenly burst into laughter. "Sunny! What are you on about?" he said.

"Ask Gran, if you don't believe me," Sunita replied. "I don't see what's so funny!"

Vikram laughed again. "I do," he told her. "And I think *you* should ask Gran about it. Then you might get the joke!"

With that, he pushed past her and out of the front door, leaving Sunita feeling completely stupid. Maybe her eavesdropping hadn't been quite right after all...

A few days later, Gemma dropped in on the Standishes' with some brilliant news. She'd just stopped off at the vet's, where Matt had said that Bart's lungs hadn't been affected by the internal injuries at all, and that he expected the dog to make a full recovery. This was *seriously* good news – Gemma had been steeling herself for the worst, ever since the accident. Bart had looked so badly injured when he'd first come in to the surgery, it had been difficult to imagine him *ever* getting back to his bouncy old self. But now he could be home within a fortnight!

"Hi, Lauren," she grinned. "Guess what?"

You could hear Lauren's yells of delight halfway across town.

Gemma practically skipped back home. Since Lauren's generous offer, she'd been feeling much happier about life, full stop. The pressure seemed to have eased off Dad a bit, and both he and her mum were pleased with the new Lucy-sitting arrangement. Mary Gordon had given her daughter a big hug when Gemma told her what Lauren had said. "I'm so pleased for you, love," she said. "Good old Lauren!"

Lucy had been the only one who wasn't totally made-up about the whole thing. She'd stuck her bottom lip out in true Lucy-style. "Lauren bosses me around all the time!"

Gemma laughed. "Serves you right!" she said.

"Gemma!" said Mrs Gordon. "No need to be like that. Just count your blessings it's all worked out the way you wanted it to. There's no need to gloat!"

"Sorry, Mum," she said, meekly. Her mum was right, but she couldn't help sneakily sticking out her tongue at Lucy.

The next day at school, the four Duston girls went to their usual spot in the playground as soon as it was breaktime.

"I'd like to have some sort of celebration for Bart," Lauren said, as they sat down on the grass. "Maybe a bit of a party at my house to welcome him home. He'll love all the attention! We could make a big doggy cake and play lots of games in the garden..."

"Hey, you don't want to get him too over-excited," warned Gemma cautiously. "I think he should be resting for a while..."

"I suppose so," Lauren said, deflating slightly. Then she perked up again. "Well, if that's the case, I think the five of us should have a bit of a celebration by ourselves then – no dogs allowed!" She turned to the others. "What do you think? We haven't all gone out together for ages!"

"Count me in," said Gemma. "I've hardly seen you lot lately!"

"Count me in, too," said Carli. "I can't remember the last time we all went out together!"

"And after the mix-up I've had with Vikram, I definitely need a good laugh!" groaned Sunita gloomily.

"What mix-up?" asked Lauren. "I'd forgotten all about him – what's happening with his love-life? Married yet, or still sneaking around with old horse-face?"

Sunita groaned again. "Nothing's happening – that's the point. I got it all wrong."

"But he *was* seeing Tracie! I saw them, twice!" Lauren protested.

"Well, he's not any more," Sunita said. "And he's *not* marrying this Jamila – and that's definite!"

"Why not? Is she horrible?" Gemma asked, confused. "Are they going to let him choose someone himself?"

"Jamila's already married!" Sunita told them, rolling her eyes.

"What?" exclaimed the others.

"And your gran didn't know?" Lauren whistled. "Ouch! She must have hit the roof!"

Sunita shook her head. "No, no – you've got it wrong, just like I did." Her cheeks started to turn pink as she told them the truth. "Jamila is actually an eighty-four-year-old great-grandma, who's coming over from India to visit – that's why Gran was so excited! And she's already married to

someone called Vikram – who's eighty-seven now and definitely *not* my brother! I just got the whole thing completely and totally wrong, I'm afraid..."

The others collapsed in laughter. "Talk about the wrong end of the stick!" spluttered Lauren. "You got the wrong end of the *tree*!"

"I know, I know," admitted Sunita. "And I think my gran might be changing her mind about how good it is for me to learn Hindi, too. She couldn't understand how I knew about Jamila coming over, so I had to tell her. Now she's realised just what secrets I'd be hearing if I could understand the language, so she's having major second thoughts..." She sighed. "But in the meantime, I'm afraid the wedding's off, girls!"

"She was a bit old for him, I suppose," Gemma said, still giggling. "Can't imagine great-grandma Jamila cheering Vik on at the touchline every Saturday, can you?"

"Going for the ref with her walking stick if he made a bad decision against Vik's team!" Lauren added. "Come on, Sunita, you've got to see the funny side!"

"Oh, I do," said Sunita, smiling ruefully. "But so do my gran, parents and brothers, unfortunately. They've told everyone about it, I feel a right idiot!"

"Well, in that case, we definitely need to go

out," Lauren said. "Take your mind off the whole thing!"

"Sounds good to me!" Sunita said eagerly. "When shall we do it?"

"How about if we get together with Anya tonight and make plans?" Carli suggested. "If we let our mums know, we could go to her house straight from school and think up something we can all do together."

"Good idea, Carli," Lauren said warmly. "Let's do it!"

Anya hadn't had a very good day, over at Lady Margaret Regis. Despite inviting her to the ice-skating party, Astrid was still being her usual cool self and hanging around with another group of girls all the time. Every time Anya tried to approach them, someone would make a private joke and they'd all giggle – even Astrid, who was supposed to be *her* friend!

Anya gritted her teeth and tried to pretend it wasn't happening. She was starting to worry about the party on Saturday. Why had Astrid invited her in the first place? She was relieved when the final bell rang and she could go out to the car park where her mum would be waiting to pick her up and take her home.

When Mrs Michaels pulled into the drive, the four girls, who'd just been dropped off themselves, got up and waved at Anya. "Oh, your friends have come to see you," Mrs Michaels said. "That's nice – lucky I've got some Jaffa Cakes and Mini-rolls in – I know what you girls are like when you get together!"

Anya couldn't have been more pleased to see her best friends. She fumbled with her seat belt and jumped out of the car.

"Hi!" she said, beaming at them. "Come in! Am I glad to see you lot!"

Five minutes later, the friends were all sitting in the Michaels' spacious living room, tucking into chocolate cake and Coke. "So what's this all about?" Anya asked, settling herself comfortably into the armchair and licking butter icing off her fingers.

"We thought we'd have a girls' day out somewhere on Sunday," Lauren said. "Fancy it for a laugh?"

"On Sunday?" echoed Anya, her face falling.

"But, that's..." She thought for a moment. Suddenly, the idea of spending time with Astrid and her cronies didn't seem so much fun after all. Then Anya smiled – she'd snub that stupid party and spend the whole day with her *real* friends!

"Cool!" Anya said, finally finishing her sentence. "I'd love to come! But what are we going to do?"

"Well, that's the thing," Sunita explained. "We haven't decided yet – we wanted to plan it all together."

"Maybe ten-pin bowling..." Lauren suggested.

"Or the zoo..." was Carli's idea.

"Yeah, ace idea," said Gemma, eyes lighting up.

"Hang on, Vet of the Year," Sunita teased, totally cheered up by now. "Haven't you had enough of animals for a bit? How about the cinema?"

"Well, whatever we do," Gemma said, "the main thing is that we're all together."

The five girls looked at each other and, all at the same time, put their little fingers out and linked hands.

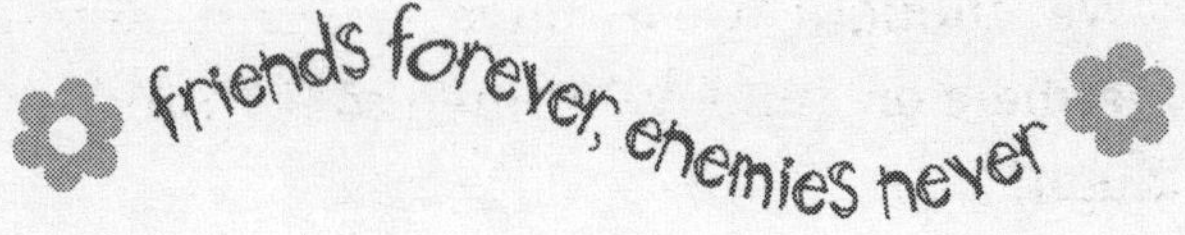

They smiled at one another.

"And so say all of us!" cried Lauren, as the others cheered.

Gemma felt a warm feeling inside her, as she looked around the close circle. So much had happened in the last few weeks, she couldn't believe it. She'd been given a big chance at the kennels – and she knew she'd really proved herself at the vet's. There was no one she'd rather celebrate with.

"Come on," she said, sitting up straight in her chair. "Let's plan something really brilliant – just the five of us. I can't wait *any* longer!"

Friends FOREVER

When Carli Pike joins Duston Middle School, she's in for a hard time. Alex Marshall, the notorious bully, is up to her old tricks again – she and her sidekicks are determined to turn the new girl's life into a nightmare.

It doesn't take the Best Friends long to see that Carli's in trouble, but Lauren loses interest and Anya is too wrapped up in her flash friend Astrid. Can Gemma and Sunita find the proof they need to help Carli survive Duston?

OH BROTHER!

The half-term break has finally arrived. Anya plans to shop till she drops! Gemma's chuffed because she's been allowed to get another pet rabbit. Lauren just can't wait to play loads of football.

But the others are seriously depressed. Sunita's gran is threatening to organise a private tutor and no one can get a word out of Carli. The holiday gets even worse when Anya's half-brother Christopher arrives. Will the Best Friends manage to hold together?

Spotlight on SUNITA

When Sunita's attention is caught by a fashion competition on TV, she knows she has to enter. Problem is, she's also got to keep the whole thing top secret. Anya's out to win too, and has wangled the perfect headstart.

During the agonising wait for results, the other Best Friends have worries of their own. Lauren goes through torment when she tries out for the district football team, despite Carli's encouragement. And Gemma? Well, her little sister is driving her *mad*...

A Challenge for LAUREN

Lauren goes pool crazy when she's selected as team captain for the annual swimming gala. But any celebrations are cut short when troublemaker Alex Marshall sets out to steal her place.

All the others want to help, but are never around at the right time. Gemma, Carli and Sunita land in trouble when a helping hand turns sour and Anya's swamped by unwanted clothes! Will the Best Friends be there when Lauren needs them most?